HENRIETTA
Goes West

HENRIETTA
Goes West

RUTH CHRISTOFFER CARLSEN

Illustrated by Wallace Tripp

1 9 6 6

HOUGHTON MIFFLIN COMPANY BOSTON

Also by Ruth Christoffer Carlsen

MR. PUDGINS

CONTENTS

We Meet Henrietta

WELL, we'd made it — we were actually on the train — all three of us. Somehow it had seemed such a wild, impossible kind of thing that we knew it couldn't possibly happen. It's a strange and very real fact that you can almost convince yourself that a thing won't happen simply because you don't want it to. But there we were. The wheels of the train kept going clackety clack, clackety clack — the scenery kept moving right by — and we kept moving on towards our very surprising destination.

I glanced out of the corner of my eye toward Jenny. She's my eight-year-old sister. And I felt a lump come up in my throat. She looked awful little there, curled up on the double seats — her thumb was in her mouth and her blanket was clutched tight against her chest. Her pigtails sure looked mighty scraggly, but I hadn't learned to do those very well as yet. Well, you can't learn everything at once, can you?

I'm Chris — Christopher Nelson — age twelve and suddenly the head of the family. At least that's what some dopey adults keep telling me. How can I be the head of the family? I haven't even had time to just be me. I shifted my weight in the seat, but I had to be careful. Pete's head was on my shoulder and he was asleep. Pete's my ten-year-old brother and a live-wire. Kind of spoiled now. But then what could you expect after three weeks in a hospital? He was pooped, poor kid. We all were.

I had to sit very, very quiet. And scenery gets sort of dull. There was nothing to do but think. So I thought. I guess I hadn't really thought about anything, since it had happened. I mean I had nightmares about it, but that isn't like thinking. Not where you set out to call up incidents and face them out. It had all begun on one of those wonderful summer days — well, wonderful is sort of a pale way to describe that day. Because it felt like the sky was bluer, the grass was greener, and the flowers brighter than they have a right to be. It made us feel great. And when our family feels great they sing. And that's what we were doing. Singing.

There we were, whirling along the freeway in our new Chev. Dad was between assignments for the army — we'd just come back from three years in Germany and before that we'd spent three years in Japan, so you can see that Petey, who was ten, and Jenny, who was eight, really didn't know very much about the United States. We should have been in school, but since Dad had to report at the end of June to his new post, Mom and he decided we should spend the three weeks we had in traveling about the country and seeing where we'd come from. They were like that. They felt this was the greatest country in the world and we should learn something about it. So we'd started in the East — Philadelphia, Washington, a glimpse of New York. Then on toward the Mid-West. We were zipping along a freeway toward Chicago. Dad wanted us to see a big-league baseball game so we were going to watch the White Sox and Yankees battle it out that afternoon. We'd sung "Old MacDonald Had a Farm," "Zippidy-do-dah," "Row, Row, Row Your Boat" — I know — I know — they're kind of corny, but some days you just feel like singing and they come naturally — these old, old songs. Funny — it seemed as if things would go along like this forever. But it's a strange and very real fact that things can change in a minute. Snap! and everything is different.

Nobody saw that big semi-trailer coming against us. At least, I don't think anyone saw it, because it all happened so quickly. There it was across a strip of dividing grass, roaring along. They say the driver fell asleep. I wouldn't know. I only know that suddenly the truck was zipping across that grass, bumping and joggling. Dad tried to turn aside. But he couldn't get out of its way. That truck rammed us like a sledge hammer going home. Jenny had been sitting up in front between Mom and Dad. She flew right through the windshield — at least they said that's what she did. Pete and I had our seat belts on, so when the car went careening off and flipped over and over it was sort of like a ride at a carnival. We were all juggled up, but still in one piece. Still everything got sort of jumbled up in our minds. The ambulance ride, the emergency room, that horrible hospital smell that burns the inside of your nose. Both of us had smashed some ribs. Pete had a real shiner where a book had caught him in the eye. And poor old Jenny had a bad skull fracture. She looked like she'd been beaten by a hammer. But she was all right — I mean it would take time, but she was all right.

And there we were. Pete, Jenny, and I all in one room, sort of dormitory style. But they wouldn't ever tell us about the folks. You know how cagey adults can be. They'd just smile or sometimes look worried, but they'd never say right out. One of the doctors said they were fine, but somehow I knew that he was lying. I guess it was when one of our regular nurses came in with her eyes all funny, sort of red rimmed like she'd really been bawling, that a funny little fear grabbed hold of my heart. I felt this cold sweat on my forehead and I wanted to scream at her. But it wouldn't have done any good. She wouldn't look at any of us. She just sniffled through taking our temperatures. I tell you I could feel myself getting scareder and scareder.

Pete snorted and shifted in the seat beside me. I could feel my neck getting stiff from having to hold it so careful like. But I couldn't move. He needed to sleep. There they were, both sleeping and I wanted to sleep too. But all I could do was think. And I thought of that morning when Captain Morris came into the room. He was one of Dad's best friends and I knew he was supposed to be in Germany. So right there I had goosebumps on my goosebumps. I knew what must be coming. That's because I was older. They wouldn't send for Captain Morris unless it was

bad. Only I didn't realize just how bad. He sort of sa-
luted me and he had the most unhappy look on his
face that you can imagine. He didn't try to pretend,
either. I mean, that's the nice thing about certain
adults. They treat you like people. I knew he must
feel pretty bad. And after he told me, I could sure see
why. That accident had killed both Mom and Dad.
And there we were. One moment a real family and
then suddenly hardly a family at all. But I couldn't
cry. Petey did. He bawled. He just let 'er rip, and I
think maybe his was the better way. But Jenny didn't
cry. She didn't say anything. She just reached for a

blanket and began to suck her thumb. I hadn't seen her do that for years — not since she had started school. She was sort of retreating from us and that scared me too.

But worst of all was the agony of wondering what would happen to the three of us. Dad and Mom were both only children. They had always said that was why they'd had the three of us. At that moment I was sort of glad they had, though there had been times that I thought they'd made an awful mistake having Pete and Jenny when they could have concentrated on just me. I knew Captain Morris had no family at all, neither wife nor children, so there wasn't much hope he was going to take us. Funny thing, we had no grandparents either. I sort of got another one of those cold sweats thinking of an orphanage. I didn't have any real picture of what an orphanage might be like, but somehow I felt it must be pretty dreary.

Jenny cried out across the aisle. The sound made me jump and I looked at her to see if she needed me. Nope. Must have been a bad dream or maybe her head ached. The train wheels kept going clackety clack, clackety clack. They had a nice sound, but today they couldn't put me to sleep. I felt as if maybe I was never going to really sleep again.

Captain Morris had more to say to us than just telling us about Mom and Dad. Jeepers, but he found it hard to get out. I think if he could have wished himself out of that room at that minute, he would have done so. There he was with Petey bawling, Jenny

sucking away on her thumb, and me staring at him.
But finally he got the words out. My mother's Aunt
Em and Uncle Elmer had agreed to take us all on a
trial basis for the summer, so we could be together
as a family. I suppose we should have been grateful,
but it's funny how you can't always drag out the right
emotions. I couldn't feel one ounce of gratitude. I
just sort of felt mad at the world. Why did it have
to happen to us? Why hadn't it happened to some
other family? We needed our Mom and Dad and
not some crazy old — and I do mean old — why
they were old enough to be our grandparents — some
crazy old aunt and uncle who were just not going to
do. How kind of them to take us on "trial." It made
me feel like a piece of equipment or maybe a sample
of hair oil. If they didn't like us, they'd return us —
with thanks. Well, maybe we wouldn't like them.
Oh, I'd heard Mom talk of her Aunt Em and Uncle
Elmer and they sounded like real kooks. They lived
in this little Iowa town and I never could figure out
what they did for a living. But I can remember all of
us hooting and hollering when she described some of
Uncle Elmer's wild inventions. He was an inventor on
the side. They keep saying if you build a better
mousetrap the world will beat a path to your door. I
hadn't heard of any great path being beaten to Uncle
Elmer's door. I guess he must not be very good with
mousetraps. And I grinned a little to myself.

Then I frowned, because what in the world did I
have to smile about? But a strange and very real fact

is that you can't go around frowning all the time. Somehow your face won't fit those lines very well. And even though it was kind of crazy, I felt better even for that tiny smile.

So I shifted sideways in the seat. It must have been more of a shift than I thought, because all of a sudden Pete's head jerked up. "Are we there?"

What a scrubby bunch of kids we were. The barber had trimmed Pete's hair so that it had a bowl-like shape. With stiff brown hair like that it really bulged on his head. I jerked my wandering thoughts back to his question. "Almost, I guess. Lean over and wake up Jenny. With the suitcases we have to carry, we can't possibly carry her too. So get her awake. You know what I mean?"

Pete nodded, jumped to his feet and started shaking Jenny like he was trying to shake her brains down into her feet. He really went at it. And Jenny went at it too. With both lungs. She hollered. She screamed. And then she started to cry. What a hullabaloo! I tell you even the conductor thought someone was getting murdered in our car. It took a bit of doing to get Jenny calmed down. But it was a funny thing. She had hollered all right. But she had never said one word. It was all sound, but not sound with words. And music may be okay with just sound, but human voices — well, they should speak words. And there's a strange and very real fact.

After Jenny had stopped her yowling, I shook her into a sweater. I know, I know, it was almost July and maybe she didn't really need that sweater, but I felt as if I had to do something to show I was looking after her. The brakeman stuck his head in the door and yelled, "Next stop, Prairie Junction."

My heart began to pound. This was it then. We couldn't back out now. I handed two packages to Jenny to carry. For a moment I thought she was going to argue with me about it. And I would have been glad for that. But no — she looked at me, then took the packages without a word, carefully putting her blanket on top where she could feel it. Pete took two small suitcases and I juggled the big ones out of the luggage rack at the end of the aisle. We stood there, waiting near the door. The wheels began the slow-down, the clacking rhythm was broken — we jerked a bit. Jenny looked a little crazy with her pigtails stuck out crooked on each side. They were straw colored and the way I'd tied them up they looked more like straw than hair. She had Mom's dark blue eyes and they were sure troubled eyes now. But that Pete he was sort of humming to himself and bouncing about. He had the kind of brown eyes that glinted. Mom used to say they glinted with mischief. Now there's a crazy idea for you. But his eyes did send off bright sparks and as for mischief — Pete didn't even have to think about mischief. He just fell into it.

The train made up its mind to stop so suddenly that Pete stumbled and kerplunk! he and Jenny were down in a heap. I had to brace myself not to follow on top of them. Pete had the breath knocked out of

him. And since we both shared the misery of cracked
ribs, I could imagine that he was getting a few mean
twinges. But he just laughed. He laughed and laughed
sitting there in the middle of the aisle until Jenny,
who had her face all screwed up to cry, began
to laugh too. Then the grownups in the seats started
to laugh. We sounded like a car-load of happy
nuts. If possible Pete and Jenny were a little messier
than before, but heck! after you get so far in messi-
ness a little more hardly shows.

"PRAIRIE JUNCTION!" shouted the brakeman,
right full in our faces. Since we were the only ones
getting off, why was he shouting? Oh, I suppose it's
the rules. Grownups always manage to have lots of
rules. Like the army, f'rinstance. Dad used to say.
. . . No, no, Chris, stop thinking of that. No point
getting all sad again. Better get off the train.

We had to sort of leap to make it onto the platform.
Seemed to me that the brakeman heaved a sigh as if
he was grateful to have gotten us this far. He waved
at a couple standing way down the platform. My
heart sank. So these were the Pufferdinks. They
looked as crazy as their name. Aunt Em and Uncle
Elmer to us. Aunt Em was all bustle and deter-
mination. I mean, I had a feeling just looking at the
set of her jaw that if she said she'd scale the Em-
pire State Building, by gum, she'd scale that
building — straight up the outside. Now Uncle Elmer looked apologetic. His face had that unassembled
look that faces get when they're made up of odd parts.

His nose was big — humped up a bit in the middle — his gray hair was cut short in a crew cut — for heaven's sakes. And he sort of ambled, as if his feet didn't know if the rest of him was coming along. You sure wouldn't get that feeling about Aunt Em.

Before she really got close enough for talking, Aunt Em began saying, "So you're the Nelson kids."

"Yes, Ma'am." That was me. I thought somebody better say something.

"Look at that, Elmer . . ." Jenny moved closer to me and grabbed the bottom of my shirt with her free hand and sort of clung there. "Doesn't that little one look like Molly? Spittin' image." Molly was my mother and just hearing her name like that brought the old lump into my throat. I guess I wasn't as tough as I thought.

"You're Chris? Hello, Chris." That was Uncle Elmer speaking. I was glad to hear he had a voice. And he grabbed my hand and started shaking it as if he were pumping away on an old pump handle. There we stood looking at each other and shaking hands and looking some more. I liked what I saw. Because in spite of all the cragginess about his face, Uncle Elmer looked kind.

"What you trying to do, Elmer? Wear his arm out? And this one here must be Pete." Aunt Em nodded. "Jenny, Pete, Chris . . . feel yourselves greeted. Greeted and welcomed. Come on, Elmer, let's get them home. They look plumb tuckered out. Take that finger out of your mouth, girl. Hear?"

The tone of Aunt Em's voice was so severe that it made me jump. Made Jenny jump too. But she pulled her thumb out. She didn't smile, but she looked interested. And she took Aunt Em's hand without a question. The two of them led off. Uncle Elmer grabbed one of Pete's bags and one of mine and the three of us followed along where the ladies led. And jumping jelly beans! you wouldn't have believed your eyes. I couldn't believe mine. Because Aunt Em and Jenny stopped beside the funniest old heap you've ever seen in your lives. I mean, I've seen cars like that in museums and sometimes on TV, but not right out in public.

"Is that a car?" asked Pete.

"Is that a car? What kind of question is that? Haven't you eyes, boy? Of course, that's a car. Just about the best car in the world, I'll have you know. Not another one like it anywhere, is there, Em?" Uncle Elmer sounded mighty upset.

"I suppose we should all be grateful for small favors," said Aunt Em with the funniest little sniff. "One of Henrietta is enough. Any more like that car would be a national disaster."

"But it looks like a box," said Pete. Sometimes he was pretty dense. He hasn't learned that there are times it's good to keep quiet. On he went. "Looks like a cracker box on wheels. Hey, what's that funny ledge running all the way around?"

"It isn't a box. It's a Willys-Knight — about 1925 vintage. And that ledge is a running board. Now if you'll all climb in we'll get started for home." Uncle Elmer sounded rather snappish. What a way to begin our trial period — getting Uncle Elmer mad at us.

I tried to think of something to say — something pleasant. But it *was* an odd car. There we were way high up in the air. The windows were all sort of small and the side ones in the back had little curtains. Pete looked at them bug-eyed. To top it off there was a neat vase of flowers — real flowers too — on each side of the back door. You couldn't look anywhere but what you met with a surprise. Take the dashboard. It looked like something you'd see on a mechanical brain. There were about a million buttons, all different colors. I mean what in the world would anyone do with so many buttons? "Say now," I cleared my throat, "that sure is one heck of a lot of buttons there, Uncle Elmer. What do they do?"

"Lots of different things. I've got so many attachments on this here car that I can hardly remember them all myself. Just sort of putter along adding this and that. All my own inventions, of course."

"Of course," I said. I mean after all who would dream up inventions for a car but Uncle Elmer? I suddenly remembered the story Mom had told us about the auto horn Uncle Elmer had invented that played "Hail, Hail, the Gang's All Here." One day he was waiting for a funeral to pass — it was some character who was known as a drunken bum — and while he was sitting there, the horn got stuck and started tooting away full volume, "Hail, Hail, the Gang's All Here."

It made the family of the deceased so mad that they got the city council to pass a special ordinance forbidding Uncle Elmer from using the horn. I snorted thinking about it.

"Take this button," said Uncle Elmer, vigorously punching at a blue one.

"Yikes!" shrieked Petey.

"Jumping jelly beans!" I yelled right at the same time, because the back of the front seat flopped backwards in our laps and Aunt Em and Jenny flopped right back with it. Their feet came up and hit the dashboard and their heads lay right in our laps. I found myself staring down into Aunt Em's eyes, and boy! she was mad.

"Elllmerrr!" she shrieked.

"Sorry, love," he mumbled. "Got the wrong button."

And he pushed a green one. Whambo! Aunt Em and Jenny flopped forward as the back of the seat flipped into position. That seat had so much action that Aunt Em's hat slid right over her eye and Jenny got the gear shift in her stomach. She didn't say a word though. Funny, I almost thought she was going to speak. But she did look back at us, sort of wildly. I know we shouldn't have, but Pete, Uncle Elmer and I almost killed ourselves laughing.

Aunt Em was spluttering and sputtering. For a few moments she was so mad that she couldn't speak. And then the words began to pour out. "I tell you, Elmer, if this car doesn't mind her manners, it's going to be all out war between her and me. You hear? War. She's got a warped sense of humor, she has. She'd just better not start anything. This tossing me around like nobby potatoes has got to stop."

Uncle Elmer wiped his eyes on his shirt sleeve. He'd been laughing so hard that tears had come. Pete and I were holding on to each other so we wouldn't fall off the back seat laughing. Aunt Em sort of looked at us with this steel-like glare. Then suddenly she started beating on the dashboard and screaming, "You hear me, Henrietta? It's war."

"Now, Em, calm down. Of course, she hears you."

"Hey, Uncle Elmer. . . ." That was Pete again.

But Uncle Elmer was busy pumping the starter and getting Henrietta underway. He didn't hear Pete — not right that moment. But once we were out on the main street, Pete tried again. "Hey, Uncle Elmer, you talk to the car like it's people. How come?"

"Because she's more like people than some people," said Uncle Elmer. "Why, this car is sensitive. When you get something perfected to the very finest point, then it just has to be sensitive, whether it's made of metal or wood or flesh and blood. And that's a strange and very real fact," said Uncle Elmer.

I tell you that phrase made me jump. Mom had always said that. It made me feel as if we'd gotten home to our folks again. Aunt Em was still huffing a bit — angry little huffs. "Oh, yes, children, Henrietta is like a person all right. Just think of the most opinionated, domineering, nasty, stubborn old woman you can and you've got a picture of Henrieeeeeeee . . ."

But she never finished that name. And we really got thrown about. That car weaved, it hopped, it jounced. How it was doing all those things at once, I don't know. "Durn you, Em, watch your tongue," snapped Uncle Elmer. "All right, Henrietta . . . all right, old girl."

He kept murmuring little, calming, pleasant words toward the engine. I tell you it was eerie. I could feel little prickles at the back of my neck. But Henrietta did stop zigging and zagging. Jenny had shut her eyes tight and was clutching her blanket like you might grab at a piece of wood when you were drowning. But Aunt Em had her arms folded and she was really glaring. She didn't say a word, not one word, until we pulled up the driveway beside an old, two-story, white house. Then she straightened her hat, looked at Uncle Elmer and spoke. "It's getting so a body can't speak straight out anymore without considering what this hunk of metal and baling wire might do. I tell you, Elmer, I'm not going to take that trip in this monster. Not unless something is done and done mighty quick to make her behave."

"Trip?" asked Pete. He was always quick to pick up anything significant. "Are we going on a trip?"

"We'd thought of it," said Uncle Elmer. "We'd sort of thought of driving out West and seeing the sights and maybe camping. Henrietta willing."

"Henrietta willing?" Aunt Em was almost speechless. "I tell you, Elmer, that takes the cake, the absolute cake." And Aunt Em stormed into the house. Jenny stood and watched her. I grabbed her hand and, carrying one suitcase, sort of steered her across the back porch and into a big kitchen.

"You children can go on upstairs," said Aunt Em. She was already tying on an apron. "You boys have the room at the right of the stairs. Jenny is across the hall from you. Get washed quick and come on down. We'll have lunch in a minute. And don't dawdle, hear? I can't stand dawdling."

"Aunt Em," said Pete, "could we go anyway — on the trip I mean, even if you . . ." I tell you the look Aunt Em turned on him withered the question in Pete's throat.

"I guess not," he muttered, "but gosh . . ."

I knew how he felt. A trip in Henrietta would be something, you could bet. But if the car kept picking on Aunt Em, we were in trouble. Quietly the three of us went upstairs and washed our hands. I couldn't believe my ears when I heard that voice — it was Jenny's voice. "Chris," she said, "are they real? Really real?"

For the first time I felt like crying — really crying. I couldn't hold some of the tears back. There are times when you cry, not because you've got a sadness in you, but because you've got such a powerful bunch of joy, that it has to get loose someway. Jenny was talking again — thank God! Real or not, the Pufferdinks had Jenny talking again. I hurried into the bathroom so Pete wouldn't see me bawl. If only things could work out! But at the moment I wasn't sure but what Jenny might be right. What if they weren't real?

And Then There's Petunia   2

WE FOUND OUT for certain that Aunt Em and Uncle Elmer were real. At least they sure had us doing a mess of real work. Out in back of that old two-story house was the biggest garden patch I'd ever seen. Living on army posts the way I had for most of my life, I'd never seen a real honest to goodness garden. And I don't mean a flower garden, you understand, but a garden in which people grow things to eat. Whoeeee — there were rows and rows of corn and beans and peas and carrots. You name it. Uncle Elmer had it.

Now it's a sad but very real fact that all the stuff that grows is not useful. I never knew there were so many weeds. But I learned. Seemed as if Pete and I were out in that garden from morning till night, hoeing and pulling and fertilizing and harvesting. Pete couldn't believe his eyes when he accidentally pulled up some green, feathery leaves and there at the end of them was a bright orange carrot. He was so excited that he let out this war whoop that brought Uncle Elmer and me on the run. We thought he must have cut off his toe with a slash of the hoe. "It's a carrot," he burbled, "a carrot. You've got carrots hid right in the dirt there."

"Skittering skunks, boy, that's the way carrots grow.

You mean you've never seen an honest to God carrot growin' before?"

"No, sir. I thought they came in bunches, like grapes. That's the way Mom always brought them home — all in a neat bunch."

Well, I thought Uncle Elmer would burst a seam on his shirt he hooted and laughed so loud. And funny thing! Pete didn't seem hurt at his laughter. He laughed right along with Uncle Elmer. Now there's a strange and very real fact — there are some people you don't mind having laugh at you. Maybe it's the quality of the laughter. There's nothing mean in it.

After he ran out of the big "ha-has" Uncle Elmer took Pete and me all over the garden showing us what things were what. I tell you, it was full of surprises. Radishes now — who would have thought such bright red things hid underground? And lettuce — it has such a complacent, comfortable look like a bunch of old ladies chit-chatting at a coffee party. Imagine, strawberries creep along on the ground and raspberries grow on prickly bushes.

Oh, yes, Aunt Em and Uncle Elmer were real enough. Pete fussed one noon about being tired. He asked in a belligerent tone of voice about going to the movies. Boy! Aunt Em just blew him down. "Tired? Nonsense. You need building up, boy. And what you need is work. We know. When you've had a big hurt, you just have to use the big muscles to sort of get it worked out of your system."

Like lots of Aunt Em's remarks, it sort of made sense. And I had to admit that Pete wasn't having the nightmares he used to have in the hospital. He was so doggone tired by the time he reached bed at night that he couldn't work up a good whoop and holler over anything.

But then there was Jenny. She was still so quiet that it sort of scared me. I mean, Jenny used to talk up a storm. Mom complained sometimes that she got tired of Jenny's questions and chatter. But Dad said, "Let her talk. It's sort of a safety valve. With Jenny, you worry when she's not talking."

So, remembering, I worried. I asked Uncle Elmer

about it one hot noon as we were chopping and digging. He stopped for a minute and leaned on his hoe. That was a nice thing about Uncle Elmer. He didn't mind stopping to talk for a minute. Maybe he was more tired than he let on and just wanted to rest. But then again, I always felt he knew that even kids need to talk sometimes, just to get things straight. "Em and I . . ." he said, "we noticed how quiet she is. 'Course not knowing Jenny before, we didn't have too much to go on. Maybe she'd always been a quiet one. But Em said, 'No, 'cause Jenny is so much like Molly and Molly was lively. So Jenny must be too.' Yep, we used to have Molly — that was your mother, Chris" (as if I didn't know) — "she came every summer. And we loved that child like she was our own. Never could figure how things sort of kept us so far apart after she grew up. But then, sometimes that's the way life works out."

He stood and gazed into the funny heat haze that was rising off the open field across the street. I thought for a moment he had forgotten what I had asked. And I could tell that Mom's being killed so sudden like had hurt him most as much as it had hurt us. Maybe because he had memories going back so much farther that his memories had deeper roots — the longer the memory, the harder the wrench when it gets pulled up. Now there's a strange and very real fact for you. The two of us just kept standing there. I hated to disturb him, because his face looked so sad there, as he was remembering. And then it didn't look sad, it looked kind of peaceful and I knew he was back to me again.

"So don't worry none about Jenny, Chris. Em says she's hurt so deep that she's kind of covered over the hurt like skin covers over a bad burn. The healing goes on underneath. One of these days, when the hurt's a little less, why she'll start to come back. Yes, you watch — that's the way it will happen. Every now and then she kind of whispers a word to Em, as if she were trying to reach out and touch living again. So Em and her just work along quiet like, most of the time, weeding the flowers" — (that's the women's department in gardening, we found out) — "and keeping the house and cooking. Yep," he nodded as if he were agreeing with himself, "that's the way it will happen. And we'd better get moving before Em hollers at us to stop the lollygagging and dreaming out here. That Em's a bearcat for work."

The days sort of flowed along in a peaceful pattern. Aunt Em and Uncle Elmer seemed to know a whole mittful of wonderful games. I admit we kind of missed television at first. Aunt Em and Uncle Elmer thought the stuff they showed was pure trash. Oh, they had a television set all right. But it was out in the barn. Well, it used to be a barn, but now it was Uncle Elmer's workshop and a garage for Henrietta. And the television stood out there facing the corner, like it had been bad. Pete asked me one night if maybe Henrietta watched it some nights. Hearing Uncle Elmer talk about that car had us almost feeling she was alive.

In place of television we'd sit at the old round kitchen table in the evenings whooping and hollering as we played Spoof and Hearts and Animal. We got so we wouldn't have given up those fun times for anything. Sometimes Aunt Em played with us and sometimes she sat in her rocker and knitted and gave Jenny some help when she needed it. I tell you, you wouldn't believe what Aunt Em was knitting. I know, because it left me open-mouthed. It was bright red wool and looked like a wind sock that flies at an airport to tell the direction of the wind. Only it seemed to go on and on. I kept hoping Uncle Elmer or Aunt Em might say what it was she was knitting, but no such luck. And Pete got so curious he finally asked, "What's that funny thing, Aunt Em?"

Aunt Em didn't look up from her knitting. "What kind of a question is that, boy?"

"But it is funny," said Pete, not about to be stopped. "Okay. It's strange. 'Cause it's so long."

"I suggest," said Uncle Elmer, reaching for his pipe and tobacco, "that you ask her what it is, Pete, without calling it funny."

For a moment I thought Pete was going to bog down. But no, he was determined to get some kind of answer. "Okay. Okay." He spoke very carefully. "What is Aunt Em knitting, Uncle Elmer?"

"Skittering skunk, boy," said Uncle Elmer with a grin, "I thought you'd never ask. It's a neck wrapper for the giraffe at the Brookfield Zoo in Chicago."

"A neck wrapper?" Pete's mouth fell open in one of

those wide drops that made you look for the bottom of his stomach. "A neck wrapper?"

"Don't act so surprised, boy," said Aunt Em. "It's perfectly logical. Giraffes are a tropical animal. Chicago is not the tropics. When the breezes blow the young giraffe gets a sore throat. A sore throat is no laughing matter when a throat goes on and on. So I'm knitting him a nice warm wrapper. And if it works, I'll just go ahead and knit some more for those other giraffes. Someone has to look after the critters. They can't look after themselves."

And she looked firmly at each of us as if daring us to disagree. Jenny went over and gave Aunt Em one of her big squeezing hugs and her face was something to see. She didn't say anything, but she looked plenty. Because Jenny is the one in our family who really loves animals. Dad and Mom used to wonder where it came from, this sort of outpouring of love and concern for God's little creatures. Mom didn't like animals much at all, and Dad was all business with them. Training was the most important thing in his mind — I mean "Do they obey?" — that's what mattered to him. Pete and I kind of liked dogs, but our feeling was a pale imitation of Jenny's reactions. She found birds with broken wings or puppies that had been hurt or cats who'd been abused. And she gave them the kind of affection that worked like a magic potion. Oh, yes, in Germany Jenny had been like the Pied Piper of old Hamlin town — she always had a following of animals.

So now we knew where she had gotten it. Evidently it had waited a generation to catch up with Jenny. She and Aunt Em were mighty alike.

This night was a night like all nights. The bright old bare bulb was hanging down over the kitchen table. Uncle Elmer had the cards out and a pencil and paper laid handy and we were about to start playing "Slap" when Aunt Em said, "Stars alive, Elmer, I've lost my knitting needle. I know I had it stuck through the bun in my hair this afternoon. You there, child — " she looked at Jenny — "slip out to where we were working in the zinnias this afternoon. Maybe I dropped it out there."

And Jenny went, just as quick. But she was gone an awful long time. And when she came back she wasn't carrying any knitting needle. She had a cat. The biggest, toughest looking, striped tom cat I ever did see. But pretty bedraggled. One ear was bleeding and it had some big bunches of fur ripped out of the back. Jenny just stood there for a minute, staring at us. She was waiting for something. And then we discovered what. She was waiting for her voice. It surprised us all when it came.

"Aunt Em?"

Aunt Em kind of started, but she didn't say anything. She seemed to be waiting to see if more words would come.

"Aunt Em, this cat is hurt. We need to fix this cat. And it's got . . . it's got . . ." But she couldn't seem to get out what that cat had. For a frightening moment I thought maybe she was fishing for the word "rabies" in her mind. It would be like Jenny to feel sorry for a rabid cat. But she never did find the word she wanted. Instead she held that cat out toward us so we could all see. And no kidding. I couldn't have said it either. It was that unbelievable, because that cat had a wooden leg. But it turned out that we didn't need to say anything.

"Dust my duds!" said Uncle Elmer, "Petunia's back."

"Petunia?" We said it all together like some speaking chorus. We even had different tones to the words.

"That . . . that . . ." Pete was almost speechless too and that takes some doing. "That cat's no Petunia," said Pete. He warmed up to his subject. In fact he sounded upset. "That cat looks like a fighting cat. What'd you go and give it that sissy name for?"

Em had taken Petunia from Jenny and held him over the sink sponging off the dirt in his sores, and he didn't even fight her. He sure looked funny, hanging limply over her arm with that wooden leg sticking out at us like an accusing finger.

"Sit down. Sit down," said Uncle Elmer. "Let me tell you about Petunia. It's some story."

To our surprise, Pete and I found that we had been so stunned by seeing the wooden leg that we'd jumped to our feet without even knowing we had. Jenny walked over and climbed into Uncle Elmer's lap and sort of snuggled back. Hadn't seen her do that before, but tonight seemed to be a good night for a lot of firsts.

"It was like this," said Uncle Elmer. "See, Em there has a heart as big as all outdoors. She's really so brimful of love for animals that it pours out in the darndest ways. Well, this evening I'm talking about, Em was taking a short cut to the neighbors, and going through that field across the street. You've seen it."

We all nodded. In fact Pete and I had more than just seen it. We had even discussed the possibility that if we stayed — (It got harder all the time to say that *if*. Still there was no use pretending. We were there only on trial. And the Pufferdinks were old. Could be that we'd be too much for them.) — but if we stayed, maybe we could build a club house over there.

"Em was all bustle and hurry. You know Em. And all of a sudden she heard this funny crying. You know how you cry when you're really hurt. It's different, isn't it?"

Now there's a strange and very real fact, but crying sounds are different. When you're not hurt real bad, you can really let loose with the shrieks and groans. But a bad hurt — somehow you have to concentrate on it and you make only little hurting sounds. Yep, Uncle Elmer was right about crying.

"So Em started out to look for the spot where the sound was coming from. Over in some deep grass she found what was making the noise. A very young cat. And he was hurt bad. Some kid had set out a trap. I suppose he was trying to catch rabbits. Lord knows we've got a lot of them around. But instead this cat had gotten himself messed up in it. He was pretty frantic. But he'd been working and working at that caught leg and he'd almost chewed it through. He was that frantic to get loose. Well, Em didn't hesitate a moment. She just waded into that situation so mad that she could have killed those kids. Lucky none of them appeared right at that moment. She got the cat out of the trap all right and she got herself pretty badly scratched in the effort because that cat was hurt so bad that the only thing he could think was that the person handling him must be responsible. Em got the cat home and we looked it over. There wasn't any question at all. The leg had to go. 'Bout killed me and Em to do the job, but we amputated it and got sulpha powder on it and put a bandage on and then Em gave the cat something to make it sleep.

"It was a mighty brave animal. Em got it in her mind it was female and she was determined to call it Petunia. So that's what we named it. After its stump got healed, Em kept hounding me to make it a leg. So I put some thinking into the idea and came up with the harness you see. Then I carved out the leg to fit. Doesn't seem to hamper Petunia none. I tell you, I think sometimes he uses that leg to konk whatever cat he's scrapping with right on the noggin. Later, we discovered that Petunia wasn't a she cat at all. She was a he. But somehow, Petunia liked his name. And we liked the flowery sound of it. So Petunia he is."

"He's the toughest tom in town," said Aunt Em proudly as she set him on the floor.

"Has to be," snorted Uncle Elmer, "to live down a name like that."

Somehow the way he said it, you knew they'd said the same things before and that the idea gave them pleasure.

Petunia moved out across that floor, actually swaggering like some old-time pirate. He had this bandage across one eye that was holding on the ear and his wooden leg went tappity-tap-tap-tap on the kitchen floor. Long John Silver or Blackbeard would have fit him better than Petunia. He sure did look tough.

"Aunt Em," said Jenny from her spot on Uncle Elmer's lap, "Aunt Em, I think you're wonderful. And I bet Petunia does too."

"Now, Jenny," said Uncle Elmer, "let's not stop there. We all think Em's pretty wonderful. What say, we give the lady a cheer?"

And I wouldn't have believed it possible, but right there in that kitchen with the light bulb burning bright and the smell of hot asphalt and green things coming through the screen door, we all let out this cheer. "Hip, hip," went Uncle Elmer.

And the three of us yelled, "Hurray!"

And for the moment I forgot we had any worries at all — about staying on at the Pufferdinks', or their being real, or what we would do if we couldn't stay. Because it's a strange and very real fact, that there are moments when everything seems right. And this was one of them.

SOMETIMES it seemed as if we had been at the Pufferdinks' forever. The days had a way of blending
together. Aunt Em kept us so busy that we didn't even
mind the fact that we hadn't met other kids. There was
a strange quality to that period, as if we were balanced
between two different lives. We hadn't really left the
old one, that familiar warm family life with Mom and
Dad. And we hadn't really joined the Pufferdinks' life.
Now there's a strange and very real fact. Sometimes
you have to live in a void before you can start living
in the world again.

Uncle Elmer had been talking about the trip West,
well, almost I guess since the moment we'd arrived.
But funny, the conversation always got turned into
the strangest by-paths. Nothing definite was ever decided. Oh, we kids were plenty anxious to go, but
Aunt Em . . . ? First it was the raspberry jam. She
said with the size family she now had, that she had
to preserve and can things and first thing on her
schedule was raspberry jam and jelly. You should have
seen us. Even Jenny scrambled through those prickly bushes picking raspberries. I bet we looked like
we had crossed paths with the biggest fightingest
army of cats you'd ever seen. All of us had scratches
on our faces, on our legs, on our arms. But once we
tasted that jam — ummmm-um! it was so good that

we'd go through a whole loaf of Aunt Em's home-baked bread in one sitting. You never tasted anything like that bread and the raspberry jam. Then the peas had to be picked and shelled and frozen. Do you know peas come in funny little cases? Jenny said they looked as if they'd been specially zippered in by God. And then there were beans to be picked and cut and frozen. It came as a real surprise that things didn't grow in nature the way one found them in cans. We learned a lot, I tell you, and we kept busy and we forgot — forgot the accident — almost forgot we were only on trial — but never really forgot Mom and Dad. Which is just the way it should be. The hurt was gone. We could almost talk about them now without tears fighting to get out and a lump rising in our throats. All things considered, I guess we were getting healed from the big hurt.

And Jenny? Each day she got a little bouncier. Her eyes began to sparkle and she chattered on and on to Aunt Em. I bet there were times that Aunt Em would have liked to put a cork in Jenny's mouth and shut off the sound for a minute. But she didn't. She listened to Jenny as if she were hearing the biggest, most exciting stuff in the world. Maybe she was.

So that noon, we had finally gotten around to the trip again. I was waiting for Aunt Em to say, "But El-mer, next week we've got to can — " I don't know what we had left to can, but I knew Aunt Em would come up with something. But it's a strange and very real fact that about the time you think you've got somebody all figured out, they surprise you. Aunt Em stuck the knitting needles through the bun of hair at the back of her head. There they perched at a crazy angle. 'Course, we were used to this, because Aunt Em always carried them like that, so they'd be handy to use when she had a minute. So now she said, "Well, Elmer, you've been jawin' and jawin' and jawin' about this trip. It's like a virus. Once you get it in your system, you got to get it out. Only way I can figure to get it out is to take that trip. May kill us all, Henrietta being so notional, but I say let's take it."

"Oh, Aunt Em, Aunt Em!" shrieked Jenny.

"Hot dog!" yelled Pete. C636189

I didn't say anything, because there are times when happiness kind of hits me all in a lump and words don't seem necessary. Uncle Elmer and I sat there grinning at each other like a couple of nitwits who'd just found a wishing well.

"Have you thought of a time, Em?" said Uncle Elmer, very cautious like. We hated to tempt our luck. Maybe she was talking about next year or the year after that.

" 'Course I've thought of a time." Aunt Em's eyes flashed and her knitting needles bobbed like excited antennae. "You must think I'm stupid. Humph!" She let the idea sink in of how stupid all of us were to even suggest she might not have decided on a time. "As I see it," she said. She paused again. Poor Jenny was having an awful time keeping her mouth shut, but she managed to hold back everything but a little spurty gurgle. "I was thinking that day after tomorrow would be just about right."

"Day after tomorrow?" There we went again like a chorus in a play. But we couldn't believe our ears. We had to say it over again to get used to the idea.

" 'Course if you don't think you can manage to get ready in that time —"

She let that sentence hang there, and we all got the message. We had just better get ready or we weren't going at all. 'Cause sure as shooting, if we hesitated just a teeny bit, Aunt Em would say, "Humph! I can see you don't really want to go."

Uncle Elmer muttered something about, "Seems like pretty short notice."

But Pete and Jenny were shouting that they'd get ready for sure. And I wondered, as they yelled, how in heck we were going to do it.

But I needn't have worried. Uncle Elmer was used to Aunt Em's sudden decisions, I guess, so he had been tuning Henrietta up. Trying to get her engine smooth and humming along. First thing after lunch, Pete and Uncle Elmer and I got Henrietta out on the drive and we began tinkering some more. I tell you, I felt like an intern helping a doctor at an operation. Uncle Elmer would stick out his hand without even looking at me or Pete and say, "socket wrench" — or "wire cutter" — or "spark plug," and we'd scramble to find the right item and drop it in his hand. It was getting pretty hot out there. Sometimes the sweat ran into my

eyes and it didn't help things a bit to rub my
eyes against my shirt sleeve because I seemed to be
solid grease all over. Still it was really great. Uncle
Elmer would explain things as he went along. He was
sure some mechanic. Jenny came out to watch and
she would hop around polishing at a hubcap for
awhile. Why, she even washed all the windows and
used polish on the chrome. Oh, we were really getting
Henrietta spruced up.

"Suppose, Pete," said Uncle Elmer at last, wiping
his hands on a cloth so oil covered that I couldn't tell
if he was wiping something off his hands or back on,
"supposin' you and Jenny hop into the front seat
there and do exactly what I tell you. Chris and me will
kind of see what's happening out here."

Those kids didn't need any second invitation.
Funny, we'd been at the Pufferdinks' forever and yet
we hadn't been out in Henrietta since the ride home
from the train. Aunt Em seemed to have a hate on toward the car and she wouldn't set foot in it. So all this
time, Uncle Elmer had been puttering around doing
lots of strange things, seemed to me, but Henrietta
had been simply sitting in the garage. "Resting up for
the trip," Uncle Elmer had said. But we'd never been
very sure that even he believed we were going to take
one.

Now Petey sat behind the wheel, pert and sassy,
and right beside him was Jenny. Uncle Elmer reached
in and pushed a button. Jenny started bouncing as if

she were imitating perpetual motion. Up and down,
up and down, up and down, she went. I mean, Jenny is
lively but this was fantastic.

"What's the matter with her? What's she doing?" I
asked.

"Looks to me like I got a mite too much action
there."

"You mean Jenny or Henrietta?" I asked.

"Both." He grinned at me. "How do you like it,
Jenny?"

"It's . . . ittttt's . . . sh . . . sh . . . aaaaa . . .
kkky. Fuuuuuuuuunny."

"What'd she say?" asked Uncle Elmer, sort of scratching at his crazy, bristling crew cut.

"She says it's shaky — funny. At least that's what I think she said."

"H'mmmm," said Uncle Elmer very thoughtfully. He raised up the hood and began tinkering with something. And Jenny bounced up and down, up and down. You'd have thought she'd landed on a hill of Mexican jumping beans. Gradually the bounces got a little less, and still less until she seemed to be jiggling. At that point Jenny started to giggle. Then she snorted, and finally she was laughing full power. This got Petey started and the two of them haw-hawed up a storm. What characters. Uncle Elmer turned off the motor. Gradually the two of them calmed down.

"How'd you like it?" asked Uncle Elmer.

"What was it?" asked Pete.

"See, I've been reading about the vibrating beds in motels and hotels. They're supposed to relax your muscles. Keep you from feeling tired. I decided it was a great idea for a car. You could relax your nerves right while you were driving along. But I think I got a mite carried away. At the rate that seat was shaking, Em might have had her teeth shaken right out of her mouth. And she'd never forgive Henrietta that. I'll tone it down some more."

"I think maybe you had better do that," said I, getting this picture of Aunt Em, knitting needles vibrating madly in her bun as she bounced higher and higher in the front seat. I grinned at the idea.

"How'd you like to see some of Henrietta's other specialties?" asked Uncle Elmer. "'Course, I can't show them all to you right now. Like the beds."

"Beds? What beds?" asked Pete.

"Why, Henrietta makes up so there are beds for us all. You'll see."

"Please tell us, Uncle Elmer," begged Jenny. "How do you get beds in here?"

Uncle Elmer hesitated for a moment. I thought he was going to play guessing games. Perhaps make each one of us tell how we thought Henrietta made up into beds. But Uncle Elmer had that wonderful knack of sensing when you ought to simply tell folks something. "See the crack all the way along the top of the door? Goes across the door frames and all?"

I looked on the outside and, of course, the other kids studied the inside.

"I see. I see," called Pete. That Pete's pretty sharp.

"Where, where? Show me." That was Jenny.

And so Pete took his finger and traced the crack along his side as far as he could reach. "Oh, now I see." Jenny nodded, satisfied.

"There's a button on the dash in there that unlatches those sides and they come down to make an extension for an air-mattress. One on each side. Then there are poles that fasten on the roof to hold the mosquito netting. And there we are. Snug as snug."

"Gosh!" sighed Pete. "That's smart — smart as smart. Do you think I'll ever get smart like you, Uncle Elmer?"

You should have seen that old man beam. The nice part about it was that Pete really meant it. "Don't see why you shouldn't, boy. Let's rev her up and see how she sounds. Step on the starter, Pete. It's that thing up above the accelerator button. See it?"

Pete saw it and he followed instructions carefully. With a roar Henrietta came into life. And she stood jiggling and jouncing on that driveway as if she were about to take off in pieces — each piece going an independent direction. But she didn't.

"What's this?" shouted Jenny and pushed.

I don't know what she pushed, but that dashboard gave you lots of choice. And the wildest thing happened. I was leaning on the hood, looking in at the kids, when the radiator cap flew off. Oh, it didn't go far, there was a chain on it. But out of that radiator came a stream of water, aiming right at the windshield. The force of it felt like water streaming out of a fireman's hose. And whammy! it caught me smack on the side of the head. I thought for a moment I might drown, but before I could swim out of the deluge, it stopped. Snap. Just like that. No more water. I tell you the windshield sure looked clean — wet, but clean. Uncle Elmer told Pete to push the orange button. He did and the windshield wipers came on. I thought maybe they'd shoot fireworks or something spectacular, but they simply flashed back and forth like any respectable window wipers. I did think I detected a little bit of an excited note in the sound. Henrietta seemed to be gearing up for something.

Uncle Elmer asked Jenny to push the purple button, and I could hardly believe what I saw. That radiator cap flipped through the air and back in place. I was going to ask Uncle Elmer how he did it, but I never got the words out, because next thing I knew, I'd been flipped backward with such force that my ribs smarted like mad again. Uncle Elmer didn't fare any better. He was at the back of the car and when it started to move, he jumped on the back bumper. Because Henrietta was certainly moving. And not any gentle moving, I tell you, but like somebody had ignited a rocket in her engine. Whoosh! away she went. I suppose the kids had pushed something.

I screamed. I yelled. And that brought Aunt Em running from the kitchen. She took one look and began to sprint and Aunt Em was no slouch. She could run. I was so dumbfounded that I sat right where I was for a moment, trying to gather my jumbled thoughts together. Then I took off too. What a sight we must have made. Henrietta zooming down the driveway with Pete behind the wheel; Uncle Elmer clutching I don't know what and riding the rear bumper; Aunt Em racing right after yelling, "Stop! Stop, you hunk of metal. Stop, I say!" And me puffing along at the rear.

Henrietta just kept going. Pete gave the wheel a wrench and they careened across the front yard. I shut my eyes for a moment. I thought they were going to take out Aunt Em's favorite lilac bush. How they missed it, I still don't know. They lurched down the slight incline and onto the street. I could see they really had a problem. I mean, when you are backing, which side of the street should you be on? Pete solved it very neatly. He held to the middle of the road.

Uncle Elmer was shouting directions from the bumper, Aunt Em was hollering like some steam calliope from in front, and Henrietta kept moving swiftly on her way. Lucky for them all that there was no traffic on the street at that moment. Why, Henrietta didn't even pause for the intersection, but zigged, zagged and bumped up the curb, over the sidewalk and into the vacant lot, that same vacant lot where long ago Aunt Em had found Petunia. Looked to me as if they might find something again, like an accident?

That bump over the curb jounced Uncle Elmer off. He flew to one side, landing in some rag weed. Aunt Em almost ran him down, she was running so fast. She hesitated a moment as if she didn't know whether to give Uncle Elmer a piece of her mind or keep going so she could shout at Henrietta. The latter action won. And how she did yell. She was almost out of breath, but she managed to call Henrietta some mighty interesting things and none of them were complimentary. But Henrietta just kept going. Jenny seemed to be trying to help Pete steer and her help was really a doozy, because they started zooming about in a circle. They must have been getting awfully dizzy inside there. They whirled by us faster and faster as if they were in

a race of some kind. Around they went. Zoom past the
heap of trash from someone's garden — zoom past
the picket fence at the rear — zoom past the redwood
fence on the side — zoom past us gaping on the sidewalk. You know how people's heads keep switching
back and forth . . . back and forth at a tennis match?
Well, that's about the way our heads were going. Only
ours were going about in a jerky circle. Uncle Elmer
kept yelling at them to step on the brake. But Aunt
Em's direction was more direct. "Push something!
Push something," she kept yelling.

And they did. The radiator cap flew off and water
hit the windshield. Then zingo the cap whipped back
on. The back of the front seat flipped down. Whump!
it flipped back up. The windshield wipers whipped
back and forth. And whammy! another stream of
water hit the windshield. I've never seen so much action in my life. On one turn I could see Jenny bouncing
up and down, up and down like she had hidden
springs. But the expression on those kids' faces was
something to see. They looked as if they'd found some
magic devices at an amusement park. Then suddenly
it was over.

Henrietta started coughing. It was a mighty healthy
cough too. Then she sputtered — jerked. The engine
sounds died away. The car stopped way across the
field from us, right near the picket fence. We ran as
if we thought they might run away again. First thing
Aunt Em did was to haul off and kick Henrietta's right
front tire a couple of times. She shook her fist at the

windshield as she was kicking and kept saying, "You ornery hunk of metal — you showoff you — you insane heap of nuts and bolts — it's war — I tell you, it's war!" Aunt Em's bun was hanging screwgy down her neck and the knitting needles were listing at a cockeyed angle. Then Aunt Em stopped. She looked sort of embarrassed. "This car," she muttered.

With a jerk she pulled open the front door, pulled out Jenny, who had a dazed and hypnotized look on her face. "Oh, Aunt Em," she said. That was all.

"Don't you worry none, honey. We'll take care of Henrietta. She ought to be in a museum, that's what she ought. Climb out, Pete. Hurry it up. You hear?"

Pete heard all right. And he climbed out right quick. Aunt Em grabbed Pete and Jenny by the hand and started striding back across the field. She called over her shoulder, "You drive that monster back, Elmer. I wouldn't trust these children to her for anything. I've never seen the like. Never."

She kept sputtering, but we couldn't hear the words. We could guess though. And I could tell from Uncle Elmer's glum expression that he and I were thinking the same thought. "I bet this means we don't go on the trip, Uncle Elmer. I just bet it does."

I climbed into the front seat and Uncle Elmer sort of eased himself behind the wheel. "I wouldn't say that — I wouldn't say that." He kept repeating those words as if he could encourage himself to believe them if he did. As he was talking he looked at the buttons.

"Yep, I thought so," he finally said. "They stopped Henrietta's action by pushing the choke button. Poor old gal, she couldn't keep going because she was drowning in gas."

"I wondered," I said.

We sat for awhile, to let the gas drain away a bit. Then finally we bounced back across the weeds into the driveway and parked at the back door. We were both dragging our feet a bit. Because we were afraid that Aunt Em might blast us right out of the kitchen, what with her being so mad at Henrietta. But jumping jelly beans! she turned on Uncle Elmer, all cross like, which we expected, and said: "What're you two doing in here? If we're to get off day after tomorrow, you'd better hump. And I do mean hump." Which we hadn't expected.

Jenny squealed. Pete shouted like a Comanche and Uncle Elmer and I grinned like two zany idiots. "If you think for one minute that I am going to let that old bundle of bolts intimidate me — me — Emma Pufferdink, you have another thought coming. And you can just put that in your tin pipe and smoke it."

I tell you, Uncle Elmer and I rushed outside quick, before she could change her mind. Uncle Elmer put his arm across my shoulder, still grinning like crazy. "You know, Chris," he said, "it's a strange but very real fact that you can't figure out the ladies whether they be people or cars."

And you know, when you think about it, you realize he's right.

The Trip Begins

Aunt Em wasn't fooling when she said we'd better hump. I thought she and Uncle Elmer must have found a formula for perpetual motion because they just went whirling through the next day. Jenny was chief errand girl. Aunt Em kept her flying around getting this and that and the next thing for the trip. Jenny lugged in some big tin boxes and Aunt Em put the staples in these — things like flour and sugar and salt. Then there were dishes and pots and pans to assemble and pack. She had Pete and me working on the camping gear and bedding, doing things like checking the air-mattresses and finding sleeping bags and pillows. Uncle Elmer kept tinkering with Henrietta. What a contraption he had rigged up to hold the luggage. Trust Uncle Elmer not to use a conventional carrier. Nope! he'd gotten something that sort of resembled short picket fencing. Why, it was even white. He screwed this on to the top of the car. Don't ask me how he did it. I only know that he did. Still, that fencing gave Henrietta a jaunty air, like lots of perky feathers there on top. None of us had realized what a small trunk the old cars used to have. Henrietta's reminded me of an outsize knapsack, hitched on the back as it was. Now knapsacks may be handy to carry things on your back, but they've never been known for the quantity of stuff they could haul. Result? That crazy luggage carrier.

We were supposed to start Thursday morning, but you know how it goes. Thursday morning we piled up the gear and the duffel bags — Uncle Elmer made us pack our clothes in these old canvas sacks because they were easier to load, he said — and the food and Petunia's sleeping box. Of course, when you're packing for five people, you just naturally end up with lots of stuff. The amount was pretty appalling. Uncle Elmer pronounced himself, "Flabbergasted!" He kept shaking his head as he looked at the stuff and I thought Henrietta sagged a bit as if she were sinking on her axles merely thinking of the load.

"Galloping goose-eggs, Em! How you expect me to get all that junk on Henrietta? You think I'm a magician or something?"

"You keep telling me that nothing," said Aunt Em, "absolutely nothing is impossible for Henrietta, Elmer. So get on with the impossible, I say. I'm going to make lunch. At the rate you're moving, we'll be lucky to be out of here by supper time."

"If you keep asking us to do the impossible," said Uncle Elmer, "it might take a little longer. But shucks, Em — " His voice trailed away.

"That reminds me. I forgot something," said Aunt Em.

And the way she bustled off holding her shoulders stiff like an iron pipe was supporting them made us feel that we'd better keep mighty quiet. She was spoiling for somebody to start something. Uncle Elmer looked at me, and grinned a bit. "Now there's a strange and very real fact, kids," he said, "you never know whether you can do the impossible until you try. So you, Pete, climb up on Henrietta's hood. Chris, get the ladder."

I ran to the barn. "Good, good," he said when I brought it back. "Put it here on the side. Now I'll get on that and stand near the middle where I can arrange the things. You and Jenny can hand the stuff to Pete, Chris. And Pete, you shove it on the roof so I can pack it in. Let's go."

We heard the kitchen door bang behind us, but only us kids turned to look. Well, there was Aunt Em. And jumping jelly beans, she was carrying the craziest assortment of junk. She had this old, long-handled umbrella with a crook at the end, a rocking chair and a transistor radio. None of us said anything. What was there to say? If she had tried, she couldn't have found stuff harder to pack than a rocking chair with its crazy pointed rockers — and an umbrella yet? I shook my head.

"Keep on passing those things up, Chris," said Uncle Elmer. Of course, the chain of passing had stopped when we caught sight of Aunt Em. Uncle Elmer had been so busy, he hadn't realized what was happening. He turned towards me and got his first look at Aunt Em. "Emmmmmmm!" he almost shrieked her name, and Uncle Elmer isn't the shrieking type.

"Emmmm." Boy! he trilled that "m." "You aren't taking that dad-blamed rocker?"

"I'm not sitting in anything else, I'll have you know. You said this trip would be comfortable, Elmer. You promised. You said it would be almost as good as at home. Don't tell me — " Her voice got that hard edge that grownups get when they're about to let loose with ugly words or some meanness. "Don't tell me you won't take my things?" We kids stood there sort of frozen. We didn't dare move a muscle. It might make Aunt Em madder.

But Uncle Elmer began to grin. "Okay, Em, if you

say so, of course, we'll take the rocker and the umbrella and that radio. Guess we can all count our bless-
ings that you don't like TV, 'cause dust my dandruff, I
don't know where we would have carried that. Come
on, kids. Don't just stand there. Start passing the stuff
up to Pete, Chris. And you too, Jenny. Hear?"

We jumped to it all right, as if someone had pushed
a spring into our feet. Aunt Em stood there, staring at
Uncle Elmer. Now it's a strange and very real fact
that when you're busting to have a fight and the other
fellow doesn't give it to you, you're left with the feeling of jumping off a cliff. Only nothing happens —
you don't fall, you hang there, waiting and waiting.

I don't know when Aunt Em left. None of us noticed the moment that she left. But we could hear her
in the kitchen all right. From the way she was banging the pots and slamming dishes on the table it
sounded as if she were at war with the stove. And
yum-yum — the smells that drifted out that door were
sure tempting. But I guess all the banging and slamming helped her work off her fighting mood, because
she even smiled a bit when she called us to lunch. We
had finished loading Henrietta right that moment, so
it was nice timing. And we were proud of our job too.
Every last thing was neatly in place. The long poles
that supported the netting were stuck along one side.
The sleeping bags and blankets and pillows and mattresses were wedged in such a way that they held the
sacks of clothes in place. And right on top, like a
throne, was the rocker. Uncle Elmer had caught the

rockers into the ropes that lashed down the rest of the gear and it rode there like some jaunty, fantastic feather. 'Course, I admit that the picket fencing didn't give Henrietta too sober an appearance either. Pete, in shoving the stuff to Uncle Elmer, had knocked part of the fencing a little screwgy which gave Henrietta a slightly cockeyed look. But secretly, I thought it fit her personality.

"What do you think of that, Em?" asked Uncle Elmer, brushing his hands together. "Every last thing is in. And even a bit of room to spare."

"Mighty precarious way to carry that rocker, I'm thinking," said Aunt Em. "You aren't thinking of losing it, are you now, Elmer?"

"Not counting on losing a thing," he said.

"Where's the umbrella?"

"Dust my duds! Forgot that blamed thing. Well, look," Uncle Elmer clambered back up the ladder, "I'll hook it over the arm of the rocker for now. I'll stow it away tonight. But at the rate we're going, we're not going to get far. Maybe no farther than the vacant lot across the street."

"Humph! that figures," said Aunt Em. "You've never been known for getting off ahead of time, Elmer. Well, just don't stand there, everybody. Lunch is getting cold."

"Boy oh boy!" shouted Pete. "Let's eat."

And we all moved. I hadn't realized how hungry I was until I faced that lasagna and French bread. We all ate as if we were starving. And we hurried. But no matter how fast we moved, it still took time to get the kitchen cleaned up, ourselves cleaned up, and everybody into the car. Uncle Elmer and Aunt Em sat in front and we kids piled into the back. I tell you, I felt like royalty riding way up high on the wheels as you do in an old car, with fresh zinnias bobbing in the vases and the little curtains tied neatly back in place. Uncle Elmer turned on the engine and with a flourish pressed down on the starter. I wouldn't have been surprised if nothing had happened. But nope! Henrietta roared into sound and the whole car began jouncing and bounding as if it were eager to be off and away.

"Oh! oh! oh!" Jenny let out this funny wail. For a moment I thought maybe a spring had popped through the seat and bitten her. But we didn't get a chance to ask what her trouble was, because she told us right out.

"Petunia. We've forgotten Petunia. You said we could take Petunia."

"Galloping goose-eggs! we can't go racing around looking for that cat," said Uncle Elmer. He sounded cross. Well, who could blame him? Not me. Here we were perched at the starting line, waiting for the gun to pop and away we'd race. And then somebody comes up with something else to stall us.

Only Aunt Em agreed with Jenny. "We did promise, Elmer. Let the child at least look for him. Wouldn't hurt you boys to give her a hand," said Aunt Em.

So out we piled. We looked in the barn. We tried the vacant lot. We hooted and we hollered. It isn't bad calling an animal with a respectable name like Spot or Puff or Pal, but Petunia — I ask you — how'd you like going around a strange neighborhood shouting, "Petunia!" at the top of your lungs? I felt like an escapee from a nut-house. But I shouted. We all shouted. No cat came. That's the way with cats. They're so darned independent. I knew that if Petunia was within a mile of that house, he could have heard us. That's how loud we were all bellowing. Obviously, he didn't choose to come.

Jenny was getting close to tears. You could see them lying right at the edges of her eye, waiting to brim over. But Aunt Em gave us the word. "Enough is enough," she called. "That cat can take care of himself. Get in, all of you. And LET'S GO!"

"Let's go! — let's go! — we're going West — we're going West!" That was Pete. He was bouncing and shouting and smiling all at once. For a moment I thought he might explode out of sheer excitement.

Jenny was kind of quiet, but she surprises me at times. She seemed to understand that we had all tried and that that is all you can ask of anyone. She accepted the decision. Oh, not with enthusiasm — she didn't bounce and shout like Pete, but at least she didn't bawl.

Down the drive we rolled and out on the street. We had to go right through the center of town and since it was the time of day that people sort of revive from the heat on a July afternoon, the streets were loaded. At the first stop sign, I saw this kid point at Henrietta. The people around him looked at us and then darned if they didn't start laughing. From then on it was horrible. The laughter rolled about us and over us in great waves. Everyone on the sidewalk was staring and laughing and pointing.

"They're looking at us, Uncle Elmer. They're looking at us," yelled Pete.

"I'm not deaf, boy," said Uncle Elmer. "And I'm not blind either. I can see they're looking all right. But it's the laughing that's getting my goat. What's so dad-blamed funny about Henrietta?"

"Maybe it's the fence. Maybe the fence has slipped," said Jenny.

"Maybe it has. But I'm guessing it hasn't," said Uncle Elmer. " 'Course, maybe laughing gas has hit the town and they can't help themselves. Still, I sure hope they don't hurt Henrietta's feelings."

"Uncle Elmer," said Jenny, "Henrietta ought to be proud. Because people don't pay attention to ordinary cars. It's because Henrietta's something special."

"Special? Humph!" said Aunt Em. I could tell she was feeling embarrassed. Her neck had this funny red flush. "She's special all right. A special menace, I'd say."

And right then Henrietta gave a funny jerk that snapped all our heads sideways. Then she gave a little lurch and then — it was crazy, but no fooling! the horn began honking. Only it wasn't plain ordinary honking. Nope! that horn was beating out, "Hail, Hail, the Gang's All Here."

The first time through we sat there and did nothing but grin foolishly. But the next time 'round, Jenny started singing — then Pete — then me — and finally even Uncle Elmer got in on the act. We were shouting and singing and laughing — all except Aunt Em. She looked mighty grim as if she thought Henrietta was making some kind of special fool of each of us.

We got through town enmeshed in sound — mostly laughter and honking and singing. Then we turned onto the highway and right off, Uncle Elmer pulled the car onto the shoulder and stopped. "I am feeling curiouser and curiouser about this," he said. "Let's see what brought this all on."

He stepped out the door, looked up and the most amazed expression started somewhere around his mouth and spread upwards until his eyebrows lifted in one of those surprised question marks. Then he slapped his knees and hooted. "Dust my dandruff! That does beat all."

Listen, we piled out of that car as if he'd shouted that there was a rattlesnake in the back seat. Whoo-eee! we made it fast. Even Aunt Em. And then we began to chuckle and snort. Pete got to laughing so hard he had to sit down on the ground. Because there was Petunia, sitting in the rocker with smugness ooz-ing from every pore. When he saw we were looking at him, he began washing himself. Over his head the umbrella had opened up so it was billowing in the

wind. Boy! that cat had solid comfort. And with that white picket fence, the rocking chair and the lumpy mounds of gear, he looked like a cat surveying his kingdom.

"As you said, Em," said Uncle Elmer, "that cat can look after himself."

"I knew Petunia was smart. I keep telling you, Elmer — that cat is smart. But smart or not, are we going to stand here all day laughing and pointing like a family of assorted nuts? Or are we leaving on a trip?"

Aunt Em had a real point there. Fun's fun, but the trip was opening ahead as far as that highway would go. We were willing and ready to start. With little yips and shrieks, we piled back in. Uncle Elmer decreed that Petunia could just ride there for a piece so we left him in his solitary splendor. Once again we chugged back onto the highway.

The wheels started rolling, the scenery started by and the heat made us all feel drowsy after the big push of getting started. I felt myself sort of drifting away — little fuzzy feelings of sleep pushed into my brain. And then Jenny was jiggling my elbow and whispering, "Chris — Chris."

"Huh? Uh? Yeah?" The sounds that came out of me were all messed up, but Jenny understood.

"Do you hear it, Chris?"

"Hear it? Hear what?"

"Henrietta? She's talking." Jenny's whisper was like a buzzing in my left ear.

"Aw, come off it, Jenny. Henrietta's making a whale of a lot of noise, I'll grant you. But she's not talking. Go to sleep, will you?"

"The wheels are so talking. I hear them. They're saying, 'Going West — going West — going West.'"

"Shut up, Jenny!" said Pete crossly from the other side.

And she did. I settled back into the corner, wiggling to get in a comfortable position. Then darned if I didn't hear it too. Under me was the right rear wheel. And it was doing something different, all right. I drifted off to sleep with an odd sensation that somebody was humming, "Going West — going West." But then, maybe it was me. I felt very happy inside.

What Gets Stuck Does Not Always Get Unstuck ... or The First Camp 5

I DON'T KNOW why it is true, I only know that it is a true and very real fact, that whenever you do something for the first time, it has a special kind of magic. Something wonderful happens that underlines the event in your memory as if drawn there with indelible ink. And that's what our first camping experience came to be. Now none of us kids had ever been camping before. Neither Mom nor Dad had been the camping type. Add to this the fact that we were living in foreign countries and that army personnel were discouraged from camping and you have the sum total of reasons why we'd never had this experience. So naturally we kids were excited at the prospect. I suppose each of us had his own separate and very special picture of what camping would be like. I don't know what it might be like with ordinary people, but I do know that camping didn't turn out as we had expected at all. Maybe it was due to Aunt Em and Uncle Elmer being the kind of people they were or maybe it was Henrietta being the kind of car she was or maybe it was the combination of them all.

But our camping — WOW! I kind of came to in the back seat when the sun was getting that warm glow on the horizon. It was late — much later than I thought. Uncle Elmer and Aunt Em hadn't said a word for hours. For all I know they might both have been asleep. After all, you could probably put Henrietta on automatic drive and she'd whirl along on her own. Into the stillness came Aunt Em's voice, sounding pert and snappy. "Well, Elmer, you planning to drive all night, too?"

"Nope. Nope. I've been looking — trying to find the right kind of spot for us. You know I've got to get Henrietta into the place. It isn't like we could park her on the road and carry in our gear. We need Henrietta."

I knew — just kind of by instinct — that all of us in the back seat were awake, but nobody spoke. There are times when it's best to be quiet and there's a strange and very real fact. I gave myself one of those waking up stretches and felt Jenny doing the same beside me. In fact, all three of us yawned in a sort of silent chorus.

"I like that spot," said Aunt Em. "Slow down, Elmer. How can a body look for anything with you tearing along at top speed?"

"Not hardly top speed, Em. I figure we're doing about 40."

"In Henrietta it feels like top speed," said Aunt Em. "She throws in so many sideways movements that you think you're burning up the pavement. Look, Elmer — there's a grassy place. And no fence either. Pull in — pull in. It's time to stop. These children are about to collapse with hunger."

"Okay, Em. Okay," said Uncle Elmer.

He braked, turned the wheel and we jolted and jerked into a field. Because that's about what it was. A weedy, old field. We could see some trees a block or so away, but the spot Aunt Em had picked sure had no scenery. From up above us, we heard a kind of mad hissing. There was a crazy clink-plunk sound as Petunia landed on the hood of the car. His wooden leg sure sounded like a battering ram. Then he jumped on the ground and whipped off into the high grass.

"Seem's Petunia's got the message," said Aunt Em. "He's off hunting for his supper. How about a hand, you young 'uns, to help us get ours?"

And she got us organized in one big hurry. Pete was dying to go off exploring like Petunia, but he did what he was told to do. And you never saw anything happen as fast as that supper did. Jenny and Pete tramped around finding firewood and they even seemed to enjoy the chore. I helped Aunt Em unload the boxes and then started to build the fire with the stuff the others were bringing in. Lucky Uncle Elmer took the time to give me some instructions or I'd have ended with the big pieces on the bottom and no fire. I hadn't realized that doing such a simple thing took some know-how too. After a bit, I got a roaring blaze going. While it was burning down to usable size, Uncle Elmer and Pete hunted up some green sticks and whittled points on each one. This was to hold the wieners. Aunt Em had the baked beans open and heating right in the fire. Jenny found the paper plates and the mus-

tard and ketchup and buns. And we were in business
— the eating business — in no time at all. Boy! did
that food taste good! Woweee — Why, I'd never
tasted a wiener made on a stick like that. It was fantastic. Like some new food invention. Jenny had two
of them and confided to us all that she liked "burned
wieners." If anyone had served those blackened,
crusty things to me in a house, I'd have thought they
were mighty poor cooks. But outside? Now there's a
strange and very real fact, but things taste better
cooked and eaten outdoors. Sometimes you can't even
believe that you've eaten the same thing before.

I guess we ate and talked and ate some more. Time
kept going by as time will. And all of a sudden we
came to with a start and realized that it was dark. That
thing coming up over the horizon was the moon, not
quite full as yet, but still throwing a soft, magic kind
of light.

"Sooooo," said Uncle Elmer, "the ladies can clean
up the supper dishes and we men can turn to getting
the beds ready. Okay?"

And, of course, it was. Jenny and Aunt Em solved
the dishwashing problem by burning the paper plates
and utensils. And we'd eaten so heartily that they
didn't have to worry about putting much away. Pete
and I got to work unloading the luggage carrier. First
we snaked out those poles. Then Pete climbed back up
and heaved down the mattresses and sleeping bags
and the netting. His aim was a little off, so that the
third bundle of stuff caught me smack on the back of

my head. The bundle and I thumped to the ground together.

"Hey, take it easy, will you?" I yelled.

I thought I heard Pete laughing, but in that light I couldn't be sure of anything. And just for a moment I wondered how much of an accident it had been.

Uncle Elmer told me to climb in the front seat and push the white button. I guess since that wild ride through the vacant lot, Uncle Elmer didn't quite trust Pete with those buttons. So in I climbed. First I had to start the engine, because this powered the equipment. Then as Henrietta was rumbling and I was jouncing and bouncing in time with her, I pushed the white button. Well, you've never heard a racket until you hear something like that. Henrietta groaned. It felt almost as if her sides were heaving. There were grating noises. But nothing happened.

Uncle Elmer stuck his head in the window. "Push the white button," he said crossly.

"I am pushing the button. I am pushing and pushing the button," I answered in just about as cross a tone as his. Did he think I was stupid or something and couldn't follow a simple little direction like that?

"Well, nothing's happening," said Uncle Elmer. "Push it some more."

So I pushed. I pushed until the end of my finger felt as if it had found some new nerves it hadn't known about before. All the pushing was making it tingle. And still nothing happened. Uncle Elmer was pulling on the sides and muttering things under his breath.

Then he walked around and looked at the other side. But Henrietta stayed just the way she was, except for some louder groaning.

"I can't understand it," said Uncle Elmer, scratching his head as if he could scratch an idea out of it. "I can't understand it."

I could see that Pete had the tin boxes loaded back in the trunk and our picnic spot was all shipshape except for the lumpy bags of sleeping gear. "Humph!" said Aunt Em. "Henrietta giving you some trouble again, Elmer?" Her voice wasn't exactly sympathetic.

"Don't seem to be able to get the sides down. In order to have places to sleep, we have to get the sides down. And in the dark here, I can't see what's wrong."

"Obviously, Henrietta's not in a mood to play house tonight," said Aunt Em. "You know Henrietta, Elmer. If she won't — she won't."

"Em," said Uncle Elmer, "that isn't likely. We're doing something wrong."

"Maybe you got a wire or two crossed," said Aunt Em. "With that hunk of junk anything is possible. Camping? Ha, I told you what camping would be like."

"Oh, Aunt Em," said Jenny, "camping is fun. We just have to learn how."

"We could sleep on the ground," said Pete helpfully.

"Could we, Uncle Elmer? I'd love to sleep on the ground. I'd — " Jenny's enthusiasm dribbled away. Aunt Em turned on her almost fiercely.

"Wait just one cotton-pickin' minute here," said Aunt Em. "Henrietta is not going to con me, Emma Pufferdink, into sleeping on the ground. You all just gather up those sleeping bags and mattresses and hold them on your laps. We'll go to a motel. That car can't outthink me yet."

She flounced into the car. It was lucky that Jenny was holding Petunia right at that minute, or I think the cat would have been left. Aunt Em was that angry. Pete and I did as we'd been told. We gathered up the stuff and piled into the back seat with it. There wasn't much room for us, but we didn't say anything. We were getting to be downright smart about when and when not to open our mouths. And there are sure a lot more times than you realize when a closed mouth helps smooth out difficulties. Uncle Elmer was mighty provoked, but he was caught between two stubborn females, Aunt Em and Henrietta. And since he had to live with Aunt Em — Well, people are more important than machines, aren't they? He abandoned camping for that night. Back we jounced onto the highway and began to hunt for a motel. Now it's a strange but very real fact that when you are not looking for a motel there are about a jillion of them and all with "vacancy" signs. But when you're trying to find one, they vanish into space. So we hunted and we looked. The towns were small and not the kind that have motels. On we went and Henrietta's wheels were going 'round and 'round, but they weren't saying anything. I imagine if they had, they might have ground out —

"drop dead." And we were about to do just that.

Then suddenly ahead of us we saw a dim kind of motel sign. It looked as if it couldn't make up its mind whether to be a sign or not. And the motel looked the very same way. I don't think it was quite sure that it was a motel. And neither were we. Whooooeee! it was old. There was a veranda kind of porch running in front of the six units. Inside there was linoleum on the floor and that sad smell of mold and dirt that old places get. The beds were iron ones. I thought they must have found them in some Salvation Army store. And the mattresses had the wildest assortment of lumps and bumps. But Aunt Em said, "It's clean. We'll stay."

And we did. I don't even remember how we got into bed. Pete and I drew a double bed and sleeping with Pete is like sleeping with an active volcano. He's really all over you. Jenny was on a cot. And Uncle Elmer and Aunt Em were in the other room separated from us by an old green curtain hung from wooden rings. It looked as if we'd found a spot that was as old as Henrietta. Nice to keep the vintage the same, I thought to myself. And I fell asleep with such speed that my last conscious moment was a feeling that Pete's elbow was in my mouth and a bedspring was nudging the back of my knee. I heaved myself into a new position and was gone.

A Noon Picnic   6

THE NEXT MORNING we all intended getting up early, but somehow we didn't make it quite as fast as we had hoped. One thing, we had no alarm and when you get to bed as late as we had, sleeping late in the morning comes pretty easy. I was sleeping this deep sleep when whump! Pete's arm hit me smack across my face. I didn't return it with any gentle courtesy either. I just grabbed hold and heaved his arm back. Well, you can imagine, having your own arm flung back at you can give you a terrible jar. Pete woke up so fast that he was kicking and hitting out at me before I could get my eyes adjusted. And the noise of that hassle brought Jenny awake and the Pufferdinks too. I tried to explain to Pete that I wasn't hitting him. He was hitting himself, but he viewed the whole argument with such a grim set of his jaw, I gave up. There was no use trying to be logical with Pete before he'd had his breakfast. Somehow his brain didn't seem to track until it had been fueled up.

Uncle Elmer stuck his head through the curtains. He told us to stop the "caterwauling" and get dressed. So we did. Actually we weren't in a very good mood for a fight anyway. It was too early in the day. I imagine we made it out of that motel in record time. If it hadn't looked very attractive in the dim light of the bulbs, the brilliant sunshine dimmed its good qualities even more. The linoleum was worn through to the floor in some spots. The beds looked even more lumpy than they had the night before. No wonder I had kept dreaming of sleeping on ant hills. Henrietta looked mighty good to us standing out there at the front porch. And inside on the front seat, Petunia was pacing back and forth, back and forth, waiting to be let out.

Aunt Em went to the trunk and took out one big old tin. From its depths she extracted a big can of orange and grapefruit juice and a package of sweet rolls. We all helped ourselves to some of each and then we kids sat on the running board and ate while Uncle Elmer leaned against the hood of the car. You could tell he was thinking. I had plenty of time to look about at the little town we were in. It was a quiet place, just inside the South Dakota state line. You could almost see that the landscape was beginning to change. The rolling hills and lush mid-summer corn fields of Iowa were giving way to a drier, flatter land. At least that's what Aunt Em said.

"Dust my duds!" Uncle Elmer's remark was so startling in the silence that we all looked at him. He kept slapping his knee so hard that his sweet roll skittered off Henrietta's hood and onto the ground. And then he began to laugh. He stood there laughing and laughing and we sat there looking. Finally, when he'd run out of laughter, as you always do, he wiped his eyes on his sleeve and pulled out an old blue bandanna to blow his nose.

"Mind telling us what that display was all about?" asked Aunt Em. "Seems pretty early in the morning for a case of hysterics. Especially when we haven't even been in Henrietta as yet."

"Now, Em," said Uncle Elmer, bending over to pick up his roll. He blew off the dust and then unconcernedly began munching away. We waited. His jaws kept moving up and down on that roll. "See, Em, I knew it couldn't be Henrietta. Why by jigs! that car is in great shape. I knew I had to be forgetting something. So I've been going over the steps in my mind. No wonder the old gal was groaning and grumbling."

"She was sure doing that, Uncle Elmer," said Pete.

"You would too, boy, if you'd been her, because there Chris was pushing the button to lower the sides and darned if I hadn't forgotten to tell him to push the release button for the latches. Lucky she's so strong and held together. If those catches had broken, I don't know what we'd have done."

"Tied her up with string," said Jenny firmly.

"I don't think Henrietta would cotton to that at all," said Uncle Elmer. "But if those catches had broken, we'd either have had to turn back or do something makeshift like that. I guess Henrietta's pretty tough."

"You're not telling us anything new," said Aunt Em, with a little sniff. "Anybody could tell she was no lady."

"Em, don't talk like that." Uncle Elmer poured himself another glass of juice and then pointed a finger at her, scolding like. "I've asked you politely not to talk like that to Henrietta."

"Actually, Elmer," said Aunt Em — she was busy picking up things and stowing them away in that knapsack of a trunk — "actually, I'm not so much talking to Henrietta as talking about her. And you know, there's a sight of difference."

I couldn't see Aunt Em's face, but I had a feeling she was kidding Uncle Elmer, although it was kind of hard to tell. We weren't any of us the least bit sorry to leave the Traveler's Haven. Yep, that was the flossy name we discovered scratched into the sign. Yet, we had to admit that it had looked like a haven of sorts last night. Down the road we went, watching the birds on the telephone wires as they gossiped and chirped. There was a haze hanging on top of the land — made it feel sort of dreamy. And then the wind began to blow. It blew the mist away all right, but there were moments when we thought that the wind was going to blow Henrietta into a ditch. Uncle Elmer wasn't traveling any main highways. He said he liked the state roads because they took you into country worth seeing. So we saw plenty of country and very few good roads or cars.

Now it's a strange but very real fact, that when you're driving along the highway, you get hungrier than if you'd been out playing a hard game of softball.

I don't know what there is about the wheels going round and the land going by and the sun beating down that makes your stomach think of food. But mine was rumbling before it was eleven o'clock. And from the sounds in the back seat I could tell I wasn't the only one getting a noisy message from his insides. Aunt Em must have felt the same way, because it wasn't much longer when she told Uncle Elmer to stop at the next park. It was time to eat.

It was a great idea, but along state highways there aren't many parks. We were getting hungrier and tireder and it looked as if we were going to whirl along forever, when suddenly Uncle Elmer pulled into a town filling station and asked for directions to their park. Of course, it wasn't on the highway, but we were past caring about that.

And I wish you could have seen that park. It had a lake. Well, not really a lake because a sign beside it said: "Reservoir — NO SWIMMING." But it looked like a lake. Uncle Elmer stopped Henrietta on a little rise where we could look across the water. And a great big oak reared up behind the picnic table, its limbs stretching way out over the water. In about one minute flat Aunt Em was bossing us all. Pete and I unloaded the food and the thermos of water while Jenny set the table. Now that was some chore, because the wind kept blowing so hard that it took all hands to keep the cloth in place. We finally anchored it down with rocks and boxes and the thermos. Petunia took this time to stretch and snoop around a bit. We watched him clack, clacking across the park. But he kept his eye on us even while he wandered.

I tell you, that meal was anything but peaceful. We had to anchor the paper plates with one hand and if you let go for even a minute, away it sailed like one of those plastic skimmers. But we all noticed the craziest thing. Here we were facing a gale and struggling to keep the stuff on the table, but those flies — you've never seen anything like those flies. They weren't big but they were determined. We could hardly hold ourselves at the table, but the flies seemed to have no trouble at all sticking on the food. I felt like a whirling dervish, holding down the plate with one hand and swishing at those pests with the other. Aunt Em had put out raisin bread and it was a challenge to tell which was a raisin and which was a fly. Pete got us all interested in trying to figure out how the flies could bank against the wind and hold their position.

Uncle Elmer urged us to quit worrying. That this was one of God's ways to give his little critters a way to handle difficulties. But that Pete — he wasn't satisfied. He wanted to know, why? And suddenly Jenny wanted to know where Petunia was and kept demanding an answer. And for a moment, things were so confusing that Pete forgot to hold his plate. It swooped up and away with such suddenness that it caught him by surprise. He lurched backwards, dodging the plate, lost his balance and fell kerplunk on his back.

"Hooeee!" yipped Pete. His yelps were never quiet

ones and had a sound and volume designed to raise mountains from their foundations. Well, this yelp raised Petunia. And I mean literally. That cat had been balanced on the far reach of a limb, edging towards a bird. And Pete's yip lifted bird and cat right into the air. But the bird was luckier than Petunia — he could fly. Poor old Petunia went up, up, and then straight down. For a moment I thought we were going to have a demonstration of whether a cat landed on its feet. But Petunia fooled us all. Kersplash! into the water he plummeted and down, down toward the depths. I don't know when we all stood up — but we did. And raced to the edge of the reservoir. And there we stood with our mouths at half-mast, stunned. Petunia came up, splashing and struggling. His wooden leg brought him up, but he was in trouble. The wood might have floated him, but it kept him on his side. He twisted and churned and kicked up a spray, but he kept going in circles. Petunia was one mad cat.

"Do something. Do something!" screamed Aunt Em. Her demand was so intense that it shocked us into action.

"I'll get him. I'll get him," yelled Pete. And he started out to shed his clothes right then and there, because he'd had enough Red Cross swimming to know that clothes are like lead weights in the water. Uncle Elmer, though, surprised us. He grabbed Pete by the arm, and he grabbed him so hard that I thought maybe he was thinking of wrenching it right off. "You'll do no such thing," he said and he said it so emphatically that my ears sort of waved from the intense vibrations. "One in the water is problem enough. Two in the water could be disaster. You children stay here. You hear me? And you, Em — you get in Henrietta."

I stood there dazed. I couldn't figure out what that order meant. Why put Aunt Em in Henrietta? Only, suddenly, I realized from the way Uncle Elmer was loping towards the car that he meant to get in too. They each seemed to pop inside and bless Henrietta — she didn't get notional and give 'em a hard time getting started. Nope, she roared into action and the three of them zoomed past us as if they had a date with destiny. Down the hill, right to the edge of the water and then! — right into the water. Jenny closed both her eyes tight and grabbed my hand. I think for a minute there she thought Petunia, Uncle Elmer, and Aunt Em were all going to a watery grave. I thought they'd gone plain crazy.

But there! I should have known. With Henrietta, just about anything was possible. She floated. I guess Uncle Elmer had some kind of flotation material under those running boards. At least she stayed up like a crazy old barge and chugged along towards Petunia who had given up the churning and was floating around sideways, looking hopelessly at his stiff leg. Henrietta really stirred up some wake. I could see that Uncle Elmer was aiming to pass on the right side. The door on Aunt Em's side opened and she crouched there in the doorway, leaning way out. Just as they came near Petunia, the waves lifted the cat up and away. Aunt Em made a sweep with her hand, but all she got was a bunch of water lapping her fingers. We could see from the way Aunt Em turned toward Uncle Elmer and moved her mouth up and down that she was really giving him what for. Now she moved farther out — right onto the running board and they made another sweep down on Petunia, but those waves swooshed the cat in the other direction. Jenny clasped my hand hard and we all sighed as Henrietta roared off down the reservoir.

By now there was quite a little group gathered on the edge of the water. And there was lots of advice being shouted. Pete was giving out with a little of his own. And so was I. Now there's a strange and very real fact, but whenever there's a crisis, there are always a lot of people ready and willing to give advice, but darn few ready to pitch in and help in a more useful way. I wish you could have seen that pond in the next few moments. Henrietta zoomed this way, and that. She cut by Petunia on the left and she cut by him on the right. She came pretty close to swamping him. Aunt Em was leaning farther and farther out and the poor cat was getting more and more water washed over his face. We were all shouting something. Anything. Even Jenny. Then Henrietta came roaring past Petunia on the right — made the most amazing sharp turn — made another fantastically sharp turn. Why you'd have thought she was putting on her brakes to make those turns. But of course that was impossible,

since the brakes were under water. Like a rocket she roared by on the left and jumping jelly beans! just as she got beside Petunia a big wave (from Henrietta's passing on the other side) caught Petunia and floated that cat towards the car. It was something to see. Cat and Aunt Em were practically washed into the car together. I could see Aunt Em's face as she caught the water full in the face. She was surprised. And on the crest of that wave was Petunia. Which just naturally plunked Petunia on the top of Aunt Em's hair. The two of them went over backwards. I tell you, it was a mess. They looked so funny that we all began laughing — all of us standing there on the shore. But nothing kept Uncle Elmer from doing what he had to do. He steered Henrietta right back to the shore. For a moment, she seemed to be having some trouble getting her wheels back on the dry land. Pete, Jenny, and I ran to her and by shoving and tugging we got her back on shore. Then in very dignified fashion — if jouncing can be dignified — she jounced back to the spot where she'd been sitting before all the excitement began.

Aunt Em stepped out holding a very soggy Petunia. And she had this funny expression on her face. I'd thought Aunt Em would be boiling mad at getting drenched like that. But there's a strange and very real fact — about the time you think you've got somebody figured out, they fool you. Aunt Em looked dazed all right. And she clutched Petunia like she was still saving him from drowning. She walked to the front of the car, leaned over, and right on the radiator cap she kissed that crazy car. Honest! she did. And we all heard her murmur, "Thank you, Henrietta."

Jenny was so excited she ran up and patted a fender and kept shouting, "Thank you — thank you." And Uncle Elmer just stood there and beamed.

I didn't do anything, except turn to Pete and say, "Come on, kid, we'd better sweep out that water. Henrietta must be feeling mighty damp on her insides."

And so that's what we did. Sometimes you can show how you feel better by actions than by words. We only had a few moments before a real crowd gathered round. There were even people snapping pictures and it was pretty exciting. Almost like being celebrities or something. Aunt Em marched off to the ladies' room and came back in dry clothes and Jenny scrubbed and rubbed at Petunia's fur with a big Turkish towel. Oh, that cat wasn't enthusiastic about the rubbing, but Jenny was afraid he might catch cold.

After drying out the car, Pete and I got the chore of loading up the food and other picnic stuff that hadn't blown away. I thought we'd never get off. And then there we were, each in his place, except for Petunia who began to walk back and forth, back and forth on our knees. I guess he had decided to walk West, which was pretty rough on certain parts of us. Uncle Elmer backed Henrietta onto the road and we were off, with people shouting "Goodbye" — "Take care" — and some just plain shouting. It seemed to me that Henrietta putzed along that afternoon like some grand old queen. And you know something surprising, not one of us minded her taking on airs.

Riding in a car can get pretty monotonous — even a car as different as Henrietta. And then we were blessed with Petunia, who kept thumping back and forth over us until I had a feeling my knees were going to be a varied pattern of bruises and scratches. Man! that wooden leg really plunked into you. Finally, I got fed up and dumped Petunia on the floor. But that didn't stop Petunia. No, siree! he just started tramping back and forth over our toes.

Of course, this wasn't the first time that we had all felt restless and bored riding along in a car. I can remember traveling in Europe with Mom and Dad. Always, about four or five in the afternoon, we hit a time when we felt that if we didn't do something active, we'd go crazy. Oh, I tell you we had some real fracases. They about drove our folks crazy, but all at once that seemed a long time ago. I could feel those old blues settling in on me as they always did when I got thinking about our parents, so I gave Pete a neat little pinch, right where he'd feel it most. He kind of jumped and looked at me, almost as if he were questioning his own senses. You see we'd been trying to be good — really good — for so long, that I guess we'd buried our real selves. Pete stared at me with a wondering look. It took a while for the pinch to percolate through his nerves to his brain and for his muscles to react. I braced myself. But no reaction. He looked the other way. I couldn't believe it. Good old Pete. Always ready for a scrap. He must be sick.

I looked sadly out the window. Wham! I got a piece of flying elbow right in my midriff. My eyes popped and I gasped. I had to gasp. I couldn't get air. I looked at Pete, and bless me, but he was serenely gazing out the other window, innocent as a lamb. Ha! and Ha! again. I gathered my thoughts a bit. Then quick as quick, I clapped him on the head and aimed a swift kick at his shins. And there was where I made my mistake. Because instead of catching Pete's shin, I caught Petunia on his jaw. That cat was not one to take things calmly, especially after his harrowing swim at noon. His attack wasn't the least bit subtle. He simply opened those jaws and clamped them on my ankle. I tried to dislodge him and he got in some mean scratches wherever he could find a surface — my face, my hands, my neck. He got me in about every possible spot.

Pete was laughing up a storm and doing absolutely nothing to help. And then Jenny got into the act. She was so worried about Petunia — not me, you notice, but that cat — that she hopped across Pete and began beating on me and trying to pull Petunia loose at the same time. This made Pete mad because Jenny was standing on him and catching him with about every second blow that she aimed at me. So he began beating on Jenny. We really had a nice fight going. Just like the old days. In fact, we were all screeching and screaming and yelling. Add to this Petunia's fighting noises and Aunt Em and Uncle Elmer hollering at us to "STOP!" and you can imagine the confusion.

We didn't even know Uncle Elmer had pulled to the side of the road. I thought we were goners when that back door opened up and Pete and I tumbled out. But there we were on a grassy shoulder. I couldn't tell you who was winning, but I had a feeling it wasn't me. Not the way Petunia was laying it on. Still it was fun. It was the most fun in ages: wild, crazy-hooting and hollering fun. That's the way I felt, until Aunt Em and Uncle Elmer got us separated. Then whooee! did Aunt Em let us have it. I've heard some tough sergeants really lay a platoon low for some error, but they could take lessons from Aunt Em. Oh, not that she used rough language or swore. Nope. It was almost what she didn't say. She ended by telling us that they had had pretty grave doubts about their abilities to cope with us youngsters, and that this little display had certainly made them realize their original analysis had been right. There was lots more. She made me feel about high enough to walk right under a garter snake without stooping. And I could tell ole Pete was taking it hard. His face got that closed, lost look it had had when Captain Morris told us about the folks. Only this time he didn't cry. Jenny just got awfully quiet, picked up Petunia and climbed into a corner of the back seat. When I looked at her she was sucking her thumb again, and I had an awful ache in my heart. Because I had started it all.

Only, it's a strange but very real fact, that the guiltier you are the harder you work to justify yourself. And I could find lots of justification like — Well, they didn't think we were angels did they? — or — How are red-blooded kids going to be quiet all the time? — and — Adults are impossible. But the harder I worked the worse I felt, until when Aunt Em told Uncle Elmer that she was too tired to cook supper and to pull into a drive-in for hamburgers, I wasn't even hungry. When I reach a point where I don't feel hungry, I'm really sick. And from the silence beside me on the seat I could guess that the rest of our family was feeling about the same way. Visions of orphanages were floating before our eyes and it wasn't a very enticing picture.

The hamburgers might have been good. I wouldn't know. Mine tasted like thin cardboard between soggy buns with mustard for flavor. And the milkshakes tasted like melted ice cream bars. Ugh! that meal was the quietest, the most subdued affair I've ever been at. Every now and then Jenny would sniff. She didn't actually cry, but she was sniffing hard in order not to. And Petunia seemed to be eating most of her food. Aunt Em and Uncle Elmer hardly spoke a word either. And the conversational tempo didn't pick up when we reached a camp spot. Each of us did what he was told. Last night we'd been tiptoe with excitement — hardly able to wait to get Henrietta made up into beds. But tonight all the tinsel had been wiped off our excitement by despair. We felt awful.

So we pushed the right buttons. Pete got out the mattresses and blankets and pillows. The back of the front seat went down to make one big level sleeping place. Then each side neatly came down to make beds for the rest of us. We blew up the mattresses and put them in place: put in the poles to support the mosquito netting and draped the white mesh across them. Oh yes, we did what we were told and said never a word.

It surely is the certain truth that at a moment when

a few right words would make everyone happy, nobody can get a word out. But at other times, when no words would be best, a million come tumbling forth. I knew I wanted to say how sorry I was to have started the trouble. But I couldn't say the words to Aunt Em. And she may have wanted to say something kind to us. Only she didn't. We didn't even tell Uncle Elmer how wonderful his invention of the sides of the car making into beds was. I knew how pleased it would make him. But I couldn't get a word past that big lump in my throat.

So we boys went over to a clump of bushes and got into our pajamas and washed in the stream and brushed our teeth. Aunt Em told us what to do. She helped Jenny. But there wasn't much kindness in her helping. Each action seemed to be overlaid with a sort of feeling of duty. Jenny drooped more and more. Aunt Em and Uncle Elmer slept in the center on the cushion part. I slept on one folded-down side and Jenny and Pete slept on the other. I could hear Jenny working on her thumb. It was a gaspy sound at times. And I almost thought I heard Pete crying. Only I was wrong, because I suddenly realized it was me crying. I hadn't cried when Mom and Dad were killed. Not once. But here were funny wet things plopping down my cheeks. I rubbed at them hard. And then on my shoulder I felt a big rough old hand. Uncle Elmer didn't say anything — not with words — but that hand patted me. And I felt he was telling me not to worry. I gulped in some air. Scrubbed harder at my eyes and was asleep.

I don't know how long I slept. I slept with that exhaustion you feel when you've used up every ounce of your strength in some hard physical activity. I bet I was even snoring. And then . . . if an atom explosion had gone off in the next field, I couldn't have been more scared. The sounds that burst over me were a combination of the Battle of the Bulge and Black Sambo's tigers fighting it out. My hair stood straight up at attention. But before I could get myself organized, I

felt myself slipping. An earthquake. It must be an earthquake. Henrietta's side fell down and dumped mattress, sleeping bag, and me on the ground. Oh, I didn't take it quietly either. I began yelling. I don't know what I was yelling. Maybe it was help or murder or just frantic sounds, but I really went at it. At that moment, something clunked me on the head. That was Petunia racing into the darkness towards safety.

The noise began to fade a bit. At least I think it did. But something was shaking my shoulder and my head was bobbing. I decided to take a look. In the moonlight I could see Aunt Em. She seemed to have both Pete and Jenny in her arms. I couldn't figure out whether she was trying to rock them or hit their heads together. But the sounds from that direction were toning down. Uncle Elmer was energetically shaking me. My words came out jiggled and bouncy. "Whaat . . . tt ha . . ha . . pp . . ened." There it was out.

"Elmer! Stop it." Aunt Em sounded half cross, half amused. "You trying to shake his brains loose?"

"Now, Em. No such thing. Just shaking them down a bit. He's been yelling so hard, I thought he'd probably lifted them out of place. Whoooeee! You kids all have good strong pairs of lungs. Let me tell you, if we were attacking the Indians tonight, they'd been scared clean to the ocean."

Pete began to giggle. Then Jenny began to giggle and before you could say "Jumping Jehoshaphat" we were all laughing. I don't know why we were laughing, but sitting out there in the middle of nowhere, shrieking and laughing seemed right. When things quieted a bit, Uncle Elmer said, "I'm sure sorry, kids. I think Petunia must have hit the alarm button. He was pretty restless tonight and probably swatted it with his wooden leg."

"Alarm button? That awful racket was an alarm?" I asked. "I guess it did sound a bit like an air-raid warning at that."

"No, no," said Uncle Elmer. "Those alarming sounds were Jenny and Pete. Dust my duds! you didn't think that wailing was Henrietta? Why, you couldn't get a sound like that out of a lady like her. No siree-bob. Nope, Henrietta's alarm is something special. When you push the alarm button, you get action, not sound. First the right side tips gently. Then the back of the front seat gives way under the middle section, dumping those sleepers. Next the left side goes. It's a progressive kind of action. I never have held that noise was a pleasant way to get waked. This way you're kind of dumped. Once you're dumped you might as well get out and be on with the day. See, you don't even have to have second thoughts. Right?"

"Oh, Uncle Elmer," giggled Jenny, "Henrietta's such fun."

"Fun?" said Pete. "You've got the wrong word. I tell you that you're not much fun to have land on a fella. I don't know, Jenny, but it seemed to me that you had four knees, six elbows, and three heads from the way they all kept thumping and bumping and banging me."

He was so serious that it made us all laugh. And we were off again.

"Well, Elmer," said Aunt Em when the laughs began to fade away, "I hope you're not planning on us starting the day in the middle of the night."

"Heck no, Em. But the alarm system is great. Now isn't it?" Aunt Em didn't say a word. She just got to her feet and looked at him. "All right, Em. I get the message. Come on, children. Let's set the beds up again."

And we all moved to help him. "I," said Aunt Em, as we were climbing back in bed again, "will take a plain old-fashioned alarm clock any day."

"But oh, Aunt Em," said Jenny. "It was fun. It was. And we're friends again."

Aunt Em stopped where she was and looked at Jenny. I couldn't see her face too well, but it looked sad and a little old and a little something else. I guess on another person you'd call it a "sweet" expression, only on Aunt Em that quality sat very gingerly. "Why, Jenny, sweet," said Aunt Em very softly, "we're more than friends. We're family. You're all the family we have. And we love you. We may get cross, but we'll never stop loving you."

I gave Henrietta an extra fond pat as I snuggled down in the sleeping bag. Bless that silly old car. She'd managed to wipe out the hurts and scars of the day before.

A Wrong Turn Is a Good Turn? 8

IT'S A STRANGE and very real fact, that you're never ready to accept the calm and dull period that always follows fun and excitement. I know we weren't. The next day's driving seemed to go on and on in dull monotony. The scenery was monotonous. Oh, I suppose the people that live there think it's great, but when you're traveling through it, that continuing dry, bleak, almost uninhabited expanse of prairie has little to recommend it. We tried games. We tried a little "undercover" horseplay — we couldn't really let go on this because Aunt Em would be madder than she had been yesterday. We tried long periods of silence. Finally we decided to try some sleep. At least Aunt Em and Pete and I decided to sleep. Even Petunia had given up his walking and was snoozing. The hum of the tires, the beating heat of the sun and the comfortable full feeling had made me drowsy. But not Jenny. She was humming and bouncing, pert as could be.

I was drifting off when Aunt Em's voice penetrated the mists of sleep closing in. "Elmer, do you know what road to take? We're not going through the badlands. Too hot and unpleasant."

I felt a little twinge of disappointment. It might have been fun to see that spot. But I could tell that Aunt Em wasn't asking our opinion. She was giving an order. No point in arguing. Uncle Elmer kind of grunted.

Then I heard Aunt Em giving Jenny directions on reading the map and telling her that it was up to her to keep Uncle Elmer on the right highway. I had this faint sensation that I ought to tell somebody something. But what that something was and who the somebody was got drowned in my drifting thoughts. I was gone.

At some later period when I shifted positions — my neck was getting stiff — I heard Jenny telling Uncle Elmer to turn left. I had that warning sensation again. I needed to tell — tell what? When you're in that half awake place, your brain gets short circuited. I grunted to myself and slept again.

Next thing I heard was Uncle Elmer booming at us about the view. View? I wondered what he could be talking about. So naturally I opened my eyes. I guess Uncle Elmer had waked everyone else too. What a strange land we looked out on. For a moment I thought maybe Henrietta had taken off and landed us on Mars. Some giant hand had certainly made strange and distorted shapes out of the sand. The sun played hide and seek through the twisted curves and cast strange shadows. It was really weird.

"Hey, Uncle Elmer, is it the desert?" asked Pete.

"Not exactly. But I've got a very strange feeling that we have wandered off into the badlands. Now how do you suppose we did that?"

And then like a sledge hammer it hit me. "Oh, gollee!" I said it before I thought and, of course, everyone stopped what they were thinking and waited for me to follow up that exclamation. If only my brain would quit letting my tongue run away like that.

"Come, come, Chris," said Aunt Em. "Don't stop there."

"It's like this." I gulped and swallowed a couple of times. I only hoped somebody wasn't going to get mad at me. Namely, Aunt Em. "You see our Dad had this real queer thing. Oh, he was smart you know." I felt I ought to say this, because actually what followed sounded a little stupid. "But Dad had this strange quirk. He couldn't tell left from right. When we took trips we'd get off in the wildest places, because when Dad told you to turn left he most generally meant turn right. Only you couldn't be sure. Mom finally made Pete and me do the map reading. Later on, when she learned to read, we found that Jenny had the same crazy difficulty as Dad. So we never let her watch maps for us."

"Merciful heavens!" said Aunt Em. "Why didn't you say something, boy? Earlier?" I had a strange feeling that she was revving up to get really mad.

"Em, Em! Don't get carried away," said Uncle Elmer. "The boy was asleep or nearly so. How could he know you were going to ask Jenny to read the map for me? Besides . . . it's a Pufferdink law. Some of the best things in life are the unexpected ones. Like suddenly having a whole family of children."

That last gave us all a warm glow. And Aunt Em

didn't say anything more. Instead she took a look around. And Aunt Em wasn't stupid. She knew right away that she was looking at something awe-inspiring. Those ridges of rocks — the weird shapes — the twisted forms of earth. They made shivers run down my backbone. And those shivers gave me goose pimples. And the goose pimples had goose pimples of their own. I don't know why, but I felt scared. Maybe it was a dim fear of that immense sweep of space and the baked, spiraling sand shapes. They sure made me feel small and unimportant. Maybe I felt deep down that this was a preview of our land if an atom bomb ever landed. Whatever it was, the sensation was eerie.

Aunt Em was the first to speak. "Well," she said, "we've seen it and I for one, am glad we've seen it. But let's push on, Elmer. This country depresses me. Besides I'm that petrified of snakes that I wouldn't want to touch a foot to the ground."

"There's a picnic spot ahead," said Uncle Elmer. "You're sure now, Em, that you don't want to stop here for supper? I hear the sunset is fantastic in this country."

Uncle Elmer was trying to be diplomatic. But there are times when diplomacy is a big waste of time. Aunt Em had made up her mind and that was that. The three of us in the back seat took a deep breath in unison, as if we were going to launch into a joint argument. But I think the futility of such an action came through to each of us. We swallowed our words. Aunt

Em whipped out her knitting and we watched her shoulder blades do a funny little jivey dance as her fingers flew at the knitting. "No, Elmer." She didn't even look at him. "I want to get out of here. Though I must say I almost expected you to ask Henrietta about stopping. She's getting so important."

"Why, Em," said Uncle Elmer very gently, "I wouldn't think of going over your head."

"EXCELSIOR!" shouted Aunt Em. It was such a crazy kind of shout. And the sound was so unexpected that it startled Petunia, who was sleeping right behind Aunt Em's neck. That cat never took things calmly, I tell you. He took off from that spot as if he'd been shot, landed with claws extended on Pete's knee. Pete let out this shriek and flung him off, catching Jenny smack in the face with a lump of cat. The sounds really exploded then and there. And right along with the inside sounds came a dull "Bloooie!"

Henrietta swerved . . . she joggled . . . she wiggled. Pete, Jenny, Petunia and I landed on the floor in a strange mixture of arms, legs, and cat parts. When we got ourselves pulled together, we found Henrietta was sitting out on the shoulder. And Aunt Em was kind of draped over the gearshift. "What," said she in an awful tone, "was that all about?"

"Why, Em," said Uncle Elmer, "it appears to me that Henrietta's just had a blowout."

"Humph!" grunted Aunt Em, pulling herself upright on the front seat, "sounded more like we were blowing up! I must say, Elmer, that you've gone over my head after all. Willy-nilly, we are going to stop. And that is Henrietta's decision."

"It appears that way," said Uncle Elmer. But he didn't sound very troubled. "You'll all have to get out. I can't jack up the car with people in it. Come on, boys, give me a hand."

"Just a cotton-pickin' minute," said Aunt Em. "You mean, I'm supposed to get out in this rattle-snake-in-fested country?"

The way she said it made me stare into that burnt-up land. I could see a snake behind each dried-up weed. Jenny began to sniffle a little. I think she was getting ready to howl. Because Jenny has a crazy fear of snakes. Why, even a little worm scares her.

"Look, Em." Uncle Elmer sounded exasperated. "Snakes don't move in the heat of the day. They move at night. And they are not going to come looking for you. Now stop this nonsense before you scare these kids silly. Hear?" He sounded so fierce that Aunt Em said in a funny meek voice, "I'm sorry, Elmer. Fear isn't reasonable. I know, when I think about it, logical like, I know you're right."

And so she climbed out. And when she got out, the rest of us didn't want to look like sissies, so we got out. It's a strange and very real fact, that if you've got something interesting to do you forget all about being afraid. Pete and I pitched in to help Uncle Elmer. Which meant moving the back seat cushion across the road for Aunt Em to sit on and knit, taking off the nuts on the wheel, and, of course, getting the jack under the bumper to raise Henrietta off that front tire. That old gal's axle really creaked as we cranked her up. She sounded as if she had rheumatism. I told Uncle Elmer that and he laughed up a storm. There's nothing like having your jokes appreciated to make you pitch in with enthusiasm.

None of us were paying much attention to Jenny, who was dragging Petunia about at the end of a leash. Aunt Em had insisted on the cat's being kept in tow so that we wouldn't have to run over the countryside to retrieve him. Out of the corner of my eye, I saw Aunt Em coming across the road toward us — probably to get some more yarn. Well, then she let out this scream. I don't know if you can imagine a scream that is part fire siren, part steam whistle and part banshee's wail. But that would come closest to describing the sound. I tell you, it about lifted Uncle Elmer and me off the ground. He was so startled that he knocked against the jack, which made Henrietta bound off into the air like a startled chicken. She bounced on the ground for a moment and then the movements dribbled away.

Uncle Elmer and I turned to really look at Aunt Em. Whoeeee! she had the funniest color in her face — sort of grayish green. She looked sick. No, on second thought, she looked petrified, which made me feel petrified. Her shriek had scared Petunia spitless. He jerked loose from Jenny and tore across the road. Well, from then on, things happened so fast that it was like watching two different movies at the same time.

Aunt Em wasn't saying anything but she kept pointing at a long, gray shadow under Henrietta's front
wheel. Now I really began to shiver, because jumping
jelly beans! right under Henrietta's front wheel lay the
biggest, thickest form with diamonds on its back. But
Uncle Elmer didn't even look worried. He bent over
and stared. Then he reached right in after it. Aunt Em
started shouting, "Don't! Don't, Elmer. You'll be
killed."

But Uncle Elmer acted as if he didn't hear her. He
got ahold of that gray form and dragged it out. Boy!
were we really shocked. It was nothing but a ragged
piece of rope, gray with weather and about as dangerous as a milkweed pod. "Merciful heavens!" said
Aunt Em.

"Do you see, Em, how you're letting your fear run
away with your sense?" Uncle Elmer sounded amused.
"There's a strange and very real fact — fear is worse
than the thing you fear. I told you that the only way
you'll see a snake in these parts is to surprise them in a
cool spot where they're sleeping."

I think he was about to say more, but I was suddenly
aware that he wasn't looking at us, but past us. "Hey,"
he said, "what's Jenny doing?"

We turned around and looked and jumping jelly
beans! there was Jenny running after Petunia, who
was streaking away like liquid fuel, straight down that
highway and trailing after him like a guide line to
home was Aunt Em's knitting. Oh, not the whole scarf.
No, that darn cat had gotten himself twisted in the

yarn and as he ran, he was pulling out the knitting. So
the farther he ran, the shorter the scarf was getting.

Aunt Em let out this hurt noise and took after Jenny.
Pete took after them both. "Looks mighty racy over
there," said Uncle Elmer, chuckling to himself.

And what a race it was. All Aunt Em's work might
have gone zipping down the highway, if the yarn
hadn't twisted in Petunia's feet and finally thrown
him head over heels, just like you've seen cow-
boys throw a rambunctious steer. When Aunt Em
caught up to him, she jerked the red yarn free from his
legs, muttering to herself. Then she walked slowly

back, rolling the yarn into a ball again. I was ready for her to blister our ears. After all, she had put a lot of time into that scarf and then to have that crazy cat pull out so much knitting in a few moments was not only discouraging, but maddening.

But there you are. Just about the time you think you've figured out exactly how a person will react they do something to surprise you. I should have been used to it with Aunt Em. But I wasn't. "Elmer," she said, "those picnic tables do look nice over there. Let's stay and eat supper."

My mouth dropped open like a trap door. "Sounds like a good idea, Em," said Uncle Elmer without a flicker of surprise. "I'm feeling a mite hungry myself."

Jenny and Pete were so pleased, though actually they weren't quite sure what they were pleased about, that they danced a jig right in the middle of the road.

Uncle Elmer began to pump the jack handle again. "You know," he said, "I believe Pufferdink's law is operating again. When chance dumps you in a situation, make the best of it."

And right then, it sounded like a wonderful idea.

Boy! Aunt Em whipped up a good meal for us that evening. Considering how she claimed to hate camping out, she knew exactly what to do with food to make it taste extra good. She mixed up three kinds of beans and chili sauce and ketchup along with some dried onion soup and bacon. Sounds weird? Yep, but it sure tasted good. Then we had fruit because she said fruit is "good for you." And then she let us have candy bars because she thought we should have something that seemed good to us too. Aunt Em was understanding that way.

Now it's a strange and very real fact, that when you're waiting for something to happen it seems to take just about forever for it to happen. That sunset must have been coming by ocean freighter from the other side of the world, because we kept waiting and waiting and the sun kept moving slower and slower down on the horizon. We had time to eat, time to pack the car, and time to do some more waiting. Of course, Aunt Em didn't waste a minute. She was working furiously at her knitting trying to get back to where she'd been before Petunia decided to give her a helping paw. In fact, she'd even had Uncle Elmer get her rocking chair off the top of the car so she could sit in comfort while she waited. So she rocked and knitted and the rest of us watched the hills.

And then it began. I can usually take sunsets or leave them. I mean, after all, it's just some coloring in the sky. Quickly gone, too. But this . . . this was like no sunset I'd ever seen. It was hard to tell where the sky ended and the sand began, because it was all flooded with color. And the strange shapes began to gain in depth and intensity until the whole landscape looked like something dreamed up by the wildest modern art painter in the world. Reds and purples and strange blues and hot oranges, blurred and blended. It was mighty impressive. And when Jenny can't find a word to say, you know you've really had an experience. Then the colors began fading. The shapes got indistinct and, much to our surprise, it was night. But not dark night, because while we'd been watching the sun sink on the one side, the moon had been rising big and orange behind us. Without even trying, we'd sort of gotten in on a double feature.

No one told us it was time to go. It was just one of those things you knew. Uncle Elmer picked up the rocker, Jenny grabbed Petunia and we started walking towards Henrietta. And galloping goose-eggs! You've never seen anything like it. Henrietta was glowing, like someone had poured some phosphorescent stuff all over her. It was ghostly. I almost expected to hear a banshee wail. But I needn't have worried. Jenny supplied that feature. "EEEEYooiks!" she yelled. That's about as near as I can come to writing down the sound.

"Hey," said Pete, "look at ole Henrietta, will you?"

"I am looking," sniffed Aunt Em. "Now what's wrong?"

"She glows, Aunt Em. She's glowing," said Pete. "Can't you see?"

"'Course, she glows," said Aunt Em. "I expect riding in her you never noticed. Well, don't stand there gawking, children. Climb in."

"What makes her glow, Uncle Elmer?" asked Jenny. "She is certainly a wonderful car, Henrietta is. I've never seen a glowing car."

We all did climb in. Then Uncle Elmer started the engine, and it hummed and purred as we pulled out of the parking lot. "It's quite a story . . . a glowing story," said Uncle Elmer. He had to stop for a moment to look and see which way to go. Then he chose to take the road to Wall. Have you heard about the Wall Drug Store? We'd heard about it even in Europe because during the war the soldiers used to put up signs telling how far it was to the Wall Drug Store in Wall, South Dakota. It got to be a real joke. I was pleased that we were going to get at least a glimpse of the place.

For a moment things were quiet. Then Uncle Elmer went on. "As I was saying, this paint job is really a funny story."

"Ha, ha!" said Aunt Em. Only it wasn't a laughing ha-ha. It was pretty snippy.

"Now, Em," said Uncle Elmer, "it is funny. You see Em was helping me with mixing paints. We were going to spray Henrietta a nice dignified black. Well,

I plum forgot that I'd gotten a gallon of this luminous paint to put out on posts — I thought I'd put these posts out near the lilac in front. Cars keep running into that dad-blamed bush. So I told Em to mix the first two cans on the second shelf."

"I did ask you, Elmer. I said these two here and you said, 'Yes.' Now be honest, Elmer Pufferdink."

"Em, who is telling the story? Of course, I'm being honest." He sounded a mite huffy. "You see, children, it's a strange but very real fact that when you're feeling the most positive, is just the time you're going to get your come-uppance. I didn't check those cans because I knew they were both black. So Em mixed the cans together as I'd directed and brought me a pail of black paint. At least it looked black to me. So I poured it in my spray gun and away I went. I tell you, spraying on paint is great sport. You have a feeling you ought to keep going and put a fresh face on everything."

"Seeing all the spots you got the paint, I'd say you'd about carried out that idea," said Aunt Em.

"What happened then?" asked Jenny. "Go on . . . go on."

I knew exactly how she felt. It does seem sometimes that grownups can be telling you the most fascinating story one minute, and the next minute they're off on something else leaving you hanging there in mid-air without an ending. But I didn't say anything. People don't like to be pushed when they're telling a story.

"So," said Uncle Elmer, "Henrietta's this nice, conservative black in the daytime. Very lady-like. But at night — especially moonlit nights like now — she gets this eerie glow. Gives you the feeling of riding in a ghost."

"Say, Uncle Elmer, maybe we really aren't here," said Pete. "Maybe we're all ghosts."

I thought it a great idea, but Jenny began to whimper. "Oh, gollee, Jenny, don't worry," I said real quick. "Nothing as crazy as Henrietta could be unreal." Henrietta swerved sharply to the right.

"Watch it!" said Uncle Elmer. "Watch out who you call crazy." His voice dribbled off.

We drove along for a little while, admiring our soft, luminous light. Once you realized it was there, you could see it. Then Jenny started humming. Aunt Em kind of tiddily tum-tum-tummed along with her. And pretty soon we were all singing. Jenny led off with "Au Clair de la Lune" a little song she'd learned in school abroad. Then Pete insisted on singing, "I see the moon, the moon sees me," and we'd hardly finished that before Uncle Elmer was leading out with "Shine On, Harvest Moon." We were all shouting and singing as you do when the moment and the people and the feel of the air are just right for happiness. So none of us was paying much attention to Henrietta. All of a sudden, Uncle Elmer stopped singing. Then I stopped because he had stopped and so did the others, like a phonograph running down. Henrietta was wheezing —

a gaspy kind of wheeze. We'd been swooping up and down hills, but now we barely managed to chug to the top of the next hill.

"Her engine's missing, Uncle Elmer," I shouted. Funny, when you're saying something terribly obvious you tend to shout.

"Oh, oh. Have we really lost the engine?" asked Jenny.

And well she might ask, because it was suddenly awfully quiet.

"Heck no, Jenny," said Pete in disgust. "The engine's still in Henrietta. Chris means something isn't working."

Pete wasn't old enough to understand that girls were always asking stupid questions about any kind of machinery. "What now, Elmer?" said Aunt Em. "We can't stop here."

"I don't think we have any choice, Em. We have stopped. But how to get us going is the problem. H'mmm." And Uncle Elmer made little thinking noises.

"Could be a vapor lock, Uncle Elmer," I suggested.

"Thought of that. Thought also of the fact that when Henrietta fell off the jack this afternoon she could have busted something loose. Hard to diagnose in the dark, but let's give it a try. Pete, boy, you get out the red brakeman's lantern that's under the seat you're sitting on. Light it up and set it back of us a ways."

"Yes, indeed," said Aunt Em. "It wouldn't be dignified for Henrietta to get hit in her behind." Somehow I knew she was kind of enjoying the thought. Uncle Elmer pulled out a big flashlight. He and I got out, folded back the hood and looked at the engine. No doubt of it. The engine was still there. We poked here and pushed there. But nothing seemed to be wrong. Pete had the red lantern flaring behind us. Seemed unnecessary in such deserted country. About the only thing that might run into us was a prairie dog or coyote and that wasn't too likely.

"No luck?" called Aunt Em. I could see her needles flash in the moonlight. She was working like crazy, knitting in the dark.

"Nope," said Uncle Elmer. He turned and looked ahead. And so did I. Off on the horizon you could see the glow that a town gives off. "Looks like Wall's not far off, but I don't want to leave you all sitting here alone while I hike in for help."

"At least there's a breeze," said Aunt Em. "It's cool."

Her remark danced aimlessly about on little gusts of air. Nobody said anything. "Dust my duds!" said Uncle Elmer, "that's it." He started slapping his knees as if he were trying to batter them to a pulp. "That's it," he said again, a little louder.

"It is?" asked Pete. He looked out into the dark trying to spot an idea in the sagebrush.

"Tell me, what do you think of when someone says 'wind'?" said Uncle Elmer.

"A hurricane?" asked Pete.

"A talky woman," said Aunt Em.

"Rain," said Jenny.

"No, no, no!" said Uncle Elmer. "It's so simple you're all missing it. Most people think of sailing."

"We do?" asked Pete.

"No, we don't," said Jenny.

" 'Course you do. Winds and sailing go together like ham and eggs."

"Aren't you forgetting one little detail, Elmer?" asked Aunt Em. "We haven't a boat, either with or without a sail."

"But we have got Henrietta," I said excitedly, suddenly realizing what Uncle Elmer was talking about. It was so logical. If you can sail on water, why not on land?

"The boys and I will rig a sail," said Uncle Elmer. "I'm sure we've got all the necessary parts. I like to come prepared, you know. You, Em, can sit inside and watch. Come on, children."

Before we knew it, Pete was standing on Henrietta's hood and I was perched on the rear bumper. We lifted off the long poles that we used to support the mosquito netting at night. Then we pulled off the tarp that covered the luggage. Uncle Elmer meantime was pulling rope out of the back seat. Even Jenny was helping, though there were moments when I thought she was more hindrance than help. We lashed the poles together with the rope and then wove them in and out of holes we poked through the canvas. It was so tall and heavy that it took all of us to hoist the sail into the air, because there was enough of a wind blowing to make it something of a fight. Jenny stood on the hood and guided the bottom of the pole into the radiator. Squish! it went into place. And squash! a fountain of water sprayed up and out, all over Jenny, who made funny little gurgling noises. Then she giggled a bit and jumped to the ground.

But we weren't finished yet. "Tie a rope on the left side of that sail, Chris, so we can control it. I'll do the same on the right. Jenny, you get in now. Pete, run back and get the lantern. Looks like Henrietta's about to take off."

And no kidding, she was. That car tugged and strained against the brakes like a boat tied to the dock. It almost made me listen for waves. When we'd finished tying the rope on the canvas, Uncle Elmer and I got in the car, still holding the ropes. Aunt Em never even looked up from her knitting, but she did give a little sniff — a very doubting sniff. The kind that says, "Show me!"

Uncle Elmer released the brake and we began to move — oh, very gently, as the wind caught in the sail. "Hey . . . wait for me!" That was Pete. Out of the dark behind us we could see this red light bobbing down the highway. It almost looked like an outrageously big and angry firefly. Uncle Elmer had to really slam on the brakes and we poised there at the crest of the hill, waiting. Pete clambered in and Uncle Elmer handed him the rope end on that side. So we were ready.

"I suppose this is a ridiculous question," said Aunt

Em, only her tone said that it wasn't at all, "but how in the name of common sense are we going to see?"

"H'mmm," said Uncle Elmer. "That is a good question. If I scrunch down, Em, I can see between the sail and the hood."

"Wonderful," said Aunt Em.

"I'll watch on the left," said Pete.

"I'll hang out on the right," said I.

"See, Em," said Uncle Elmer, "no problem at all."

And with that he took his foot off the brake. With a sigh of relief, Henrietta slipped away from the top of that hill. She picked up momentum. The sail billowed out and the canvas tugged at the rope. We really moved. At least we had that feeling. Maybe it was the terrific silence that made us feel we were flying in the wind.

"It is like sailing. It really is," said Jenny.

And she was right, because off in the moonlit fields the prairie grass was bending before the wind. It moved like waves, up and down.

"Well," said Aunt Em, "now I know what they mean by a sea of grass. It's a good description. It is moving. Like water."

Up the next hill we glided. We almost stopped before we reached the crest. Then a little push of wind from behind helped us over the top and away we went. "Uncle Elmer," said Pete, "you know something?"

"Yep. I know a few things. Like what, Pete?"

"Like we don't have headlights anymore."

"Dust my duds!" said Uncle Elmer, "you are absolutely right."

"Heaven help us if we meet a sheriff or even the highway patrol," said Aunt Em.

" 'Course, Em," said Uncle Elmer, "it's arguable whether we're driving or sailing. And does sailing come under the driving laws?" We all hooted at the idea of some policeman trying to solve that question.

"Hey . . . hey," shouted Pete. "There's the town."

But Pete was so excited about the town that he forgot to hold his rope taut. "Pete . . . you on the port side — pull, pull."

"Port? Is that me? Oh, port . . ." said Pete. He almost fell out of the window trying to get a grasp on the rope. And he got a good look at Main Street at the same time. "Rocks on the starboard side—lights ahead," he yelled. He was getting in the swing of it.

The rocks were really cars. But Pete was getting caught up in the spirit of the ride. There were only a few people about. In small towns, nothing much is operating by ten at night. I noticed a man bending over the lock at the drug store, as if checking to see if it were locked.

"Harbor lights," sang out Jenny, "pretty harbor lights."

"Hey, laddies," shouted Uncle Elmer in a booming voice. "You on the starboard and larboard pull." Which we did and Henrietta almost tugged the rope out of our hands as she sped forwards. Suddenly Uncle Elmer burst into a raucous sea chanty and the music was so contagious that Pete and I hollered the words right along with him. Even Jenny and Aunt Em joined in. "Heave ho, my lads, the wind blows free . . ." I bet you could have heard us clear to Chicago. I know for certain sure that the gang of boys standing near the street light turned to look in surprise. And when they looked at Henrietta they were more than surprised. The man at the drug store turned and gaped and then he started running after us.

"A ship of the desert," yelled one of the boys. "Hey, that must be a real ship of the desert."

"Do you see it? Do you see it?" shouted the man to nobody and to everybody and he got no answer, especially from us.

Henrietta swooped silently down that street and picked up speed. Right on the edge of town — we were almost outside it — I saw this woman in a white dress step out on the front porch. Then suddenly she was shouting — not gentle little shouts, but loud, almost frightened ones. "Son, son . . . a ghost ship . . . a ship. Come see."

I chuckled as I wondered what that son would feel when he saw our glimmering luminous back disappearing down the road with the sail billowing ahead.

We didn't go far after that, probably about half a mile, when Aunt Em spotted a flat spot, handy to the road. We were ready to quit by then. The ropes were tugging so hard on my arms, that I could imagine how tired Pete must be. Besides, it was getting awfully late. We glided into the spot. It was nice. Screened from the highway by scrubby brush and tall grass. It didn't take us long to get the sides on Henrietta down, the tarp back in place on the roof, the poles attached to hold the netting, and the sleeping bags and pillows in the right spots. And we rushed to bed as if we were after some "instant" sleep. We may have only been on the way a few days, but we moved like a well-trained army.

But after all the excitement, I found it hard to settle down. I was lying there, thinking and chuckling to myself about our sail through Wall. And just as I was beginning to drift away, I heard a couple of cars slow

down and stop on the highway, right near us. There hadn't been any other traffic since we'd bedded down, so it startled me a bit. I could hear voices calling back and forth.

"You're sure it was a boat?" asked one voice.

"Where is it?" squeaked a high, quavery one.

"It was glowing . . . ghostly it was. And there were little faces at the sides. I could see the eyes." That was another voice.

"You're crazy, every one of you. Crazy with heat or boredom or plain crazy. Sailing boats in South Dakota." Ugly laughter followed this remark.

There were more remarks. But they were all jumbled together. Finally one rose above the chatter. "Okay, okay, you guys. Do we turn here onto this side road or go straight ahead? Will someone make up his mind?"

"Go ahead," ordered a deep decisive voice. "That side road leads nowhere." The cars started up and the voices faded. Crazy idea for sure, I thought to myself . . . sailing ships in South Dakota. Then a wide grin sort of burst all over my face and I think I fell asleep smiling. Gollee! it sure felt good.

Henrietta Meets the Boys

Iᴛ's a strange and frustrating fact that fun times have to end. And no matter when it happens, you're not ready for it. The morning after our moonlight sail through Wall, we woke up with that Christmas morning feeling. "Oh, what a beautiful morning," Pete and I yodeled in our off-key harmony as we splashed some water on our faces and scrubbed away at our teeth. Brushing our teeth did interfere a bit with our singing or perhaps the singing interfered with our brushing our teeth, but we kept trying. Anyway we were feeling great — for the moment.

Then Aunt Em began complaining. She had no milk. This really upset her. Oh, not because she thought we needed milk, but because Petunia kept brushing against her legs and making all those happy purry noises that a cat makes when he wants to be fed. Aunt Em could explain to us about the lack of milk, but she couldn't get the message across to Petunia. So she began scolding Jenny for tangling her hair and fussing at Uncle Elmer for picking such a dusty spot to stop in.

And then wowee! she opened the trunk to get out the eggs. We had eggs in that trunk all right, only they were all over. Now I ask you, have you ever tried to clean up the sloppy slimey whites and the squishy yokes out of a trunk — without water? Yikes! what a mess. And Pete and I got the chore of cleaning it up. We were running low on water so Aunt Em insisted we wipe out the egg with dry rags. This made Pete and me cross.

And Uncle Elmer felt cross because when he got underneath Henrietta to see what might have caused her to stall the night before, he found this little bitzy hole in the gas tank. I guess when she fell off the jack in that hullabaloo over the imaginary snake, a branch must have pierced the tank. Anyway, it sure explained why we came to a stall as we had driven toward Wall. Obviously most of the gas must have dribbled away while we sat and watched the sunset.

'Course it wasn't any problem for Uncle Elmer to get that hole fixed. He always had ideas about a mile a minute. This time he got Jenny to chew up a stick of gum for him. Then he crawled under Henrietta again and stuck the gum smack into the hole. She was shipshape for the moment. Only we still had the little problem of no gas. I could guess what was coming. And it did. Uncle Elmer told Pete and me to get out on the highway and hike into town, which looked like a hot dreary chore without any breakfast. But I needn't have worried. Aunt Em insisted we boys eat first and what a breakfast she dreamed up. She had us chomp up some dried prunes — that was the fruit course. Then she made peanut butter sandwiches and gave us slices of cheese to accompany them. Uncle Elmer squawked a little about peanut butter sandwiches. Aunt Em glared him down. She said peanut butter was nourishing and cheese was a substitute for the milk we didn't have.

Aunt Em probably had nutritional logic on her side, but on the eating side that combination was purely terrible. I had this ugly taste in my mouth when we'd finished eating that nothing would wash away. For the moment I could think of nothing nicer than to give someone a good punch in the nose. But I didn't dare.

Instead Pete and I found ourselves out on the highway and on the way to Wall. Poor old Pete! for the first time that day I took a look at him. His hair looked like it had been whipped up in a mixing bowl. It was going every which way. Then he trudged along with such slow dragging steps, that he appeared downright pathetic. Made me feel ashamed of myself for being such a grump. But I couldn't think of any words to say. So I began to whistle. Oh, I'm not very good at whistling, but it's a strange and very real fact that a whistle does something to your spirit. Perks you up when you're in the dumps. Maybe just pulling your lips in a puckered position relieves the down pull of a frown. Anyway whistling sure seemed to help. Pretty soon, Pete was whistling too and we began walking side by side.

And right then this car stopped and gave us a lift into town. Seemed as if once we'd changed our grumpy mood for a happier one, everything began to go better for us. The gas station attendant was a nice young guy. He looked sleepy, but good-natured. He found a gallon can for us and he kept up this machine gun stream of talk, as if his mouth were operating on an automatic impulse. What he was talking up a storm about was the mysterious something that people had seen pass through the town the night before. What a description he had of Henrietta. He mentioned the sail . . . well, that was correct. I guess nobody could miss the sail. And he mentioned how the object glowed . . . also correct. But when he got to the shape it was crazy. He said the "thing," as he called it, had a shape like a beetle, oval, and there were little people peering over the sides. Then he said they were keening. I asked him what "keening" meant. He thought a minute. In fact he thought so hard he let the gas run right over the top of the can. It took him a while to get it all wiped up.

"Keening," he explained, "is a sound without words — a wailing sound." He said that some people thought there were words in the sounds, but most others disagreed.

I tell you, Pete and I thought we were going to strangle. We didn't know whether to laugh or to try and tell him about Henrietta. Wouldn't Uncle Elmer be surprised to hear that the sea chanties had come out sounding like keening? Not exactly a compliment, I'm afraid. I glared at Pete, who looked about to burst, and lucky for us a pick-up drove up for gas. Once the attendant had gone over to wait on that customer, we could let loose. We held on to each other and silently laughed. We were afraid to laugh out loud for fear we'd get everybody asking questions.

Then the attendant came back and said that the fellow in the pick-up would give us a ride because he was going our way. Which was lucky for us.

So we paid him and climbed in the truck, and then blamed, if that boy didn't start telling the driver the same story about Henrietta. But he added some details. He said the town had called in the army because they thought it might be an invasion from another planet. Pete got bug-eyed. Now we had the army to contend with. But I was sure that Henrietta could handle anything that came her way. We were awfully quiet on the short ride, and reached the cross road mighty quick.

"Hey," said the driver before he pulled off, "that's a mighty interesting old car." Lucky that Uncle Elmer had the sides up. Otherwise he might have been even more interested in Henrietta. Aunt Em was sitting there in her rocker knitting, so it all looked very peaceful.

"Yep . . . she's old," said Pete. "And wonderful," he added.

"I'd say, she was about as good as a flying saucer. Wouldn't you, Pete?" I gave him a little nudge and he burst out laughing.

But the driver never tumbled. He nodded pleasantly at us and drove away. Pete and I hauled the gas can over to Henrietta and poured in the gasoline. I thought we'd get underway right then, but nope. We might have lost our grumpy feelings on the trip to town. But not Aunt Em. She had her teeth set in mean feelings like a horse with a bit in his mouth. And she seemed to be enjoying the feeling to its fullest. She announced that we had to get some frozen vegetables for lunch. She was tired of canned things. We were to get two cartons of pop, bread, milk, candy bars. Oh, yes, a ring of bologna.

I thought for a moment that Uncle Elmer was going to be cross right back at her. But he wasn't. He said she was absolutely right. Besides he had to return the can to the station and get more gas. He knew he had to have more than a gallon to get us all the way to Rapid City. All of us kids piled into Henrietta and were off to Wall. We took care of Henrietta first and then we went to the grocery store. Hey, we really had a time trying to remember the things Aunt Em had told us to get. Everybody had thought somebody else was listening. We had to scratch around in our memories to dredge up the list. Finally, we had all the things assembled. Then we talked Uncle Elmer into letting us go into the drug store because it was so famous and all. We had our pictures taken on the buffalo and climbed up the tall observation tower to get a view of the countryside and we stopped to watch the animated figures. They were life-sized and really caught the spirit of the old West. We almost bogged down among the counters of souvenirs. I bet there were about a million different items that you could buy in that place. Only Uncle Elmer said, "No souvenirs." So we weren't troubled in trying to make a choice. He told us that he wanted us to have experiences. Nobody could ever take experiences away from you. But buying a lot of junk was sheer nonsense. At least that was what I think he said.

And while we were gawking inside at all the curiosities, Henrietta was collecting a crowd of her own. I suppose in her own right, she was something of a curiosity too. People wanted to know about the button panel and the gadgets. It took us a long time to get disentangled and on our way to the camp. Aunt Em, meanwhile, had been sitting out in the sun, rocking and knitting while we were gone. She was about the color of the red in the American flag. And I think her temper matched the outside color too. I expected an explosion, but she only grunted at us. "Well, Petunia's gone. We'll have to find that cat before we can go."

Sometimes it seems to me that we spent more time on this trip hunting for Petunia than traveling. But we didn't argue. I mean, obviously, we did have to find Petunia. Pete and I started off in one direction and Uncle Elmer with Jenny in tow moved in the opposite way. Aunt Em was putting the groceries in the trunk. And then she let out this disgusted snort. We weren't far enough away to miss it.

"Elmer. Elmer Pufferdink," she called. "Where's the milk?"

We all stopped right where we were. And this horrible sinking feeling hit me. "Dust my duds! Em," he called back, "we musta forgot it. We'll stop somewhere and get it. Come on. Help us hunt Petunia."

Aunt Em nodded. "I might have known you'd forget," she said. But there's a strange and very real fact, knowing that we'd been stupid and forgotten something seemed to restore her good humor. She suddenly was no longer cross. In a moment she followed along after Pete and me. How we hollered and shouted. If Petunia had been in the next county, he couldn't have missed hearing us. But he didn't choose to come. We must have tramped about close to half an hour with no luck. All of us were beginning to match Aunt Em's red color and we were dusty and thirsty. When we met Uncle Elmer and Jenny, Uncle Elmer was muttering to himself. He might have been cursing Petunia, if he'd been the cussing sort. Dad used to tell me that there were times that a few vigorous "cuss" words could sure let off steam.

"Well, Em," said Uncle Elmer. "No cat. What should we do now?"

"We've got no choice, Elmer. We'll have to go back to the car and wait. We can't leave him out here to die. You know that, Elmer."

"Yep, I do know it," he said. "But I kept hoping we wouldn't have to wait. Well, come on, kids, let's see how Pufferdink's law . . . what is it now?" He paused and looked at us.

"Enjoy the unexpected," we shouted at him.

"Right! Let's see what this unexpected produces. Back to Henrietta."

And he led the way through the brush. I was tramping close behind him, not paying any attention. Because when you're walking in a line like that you ex-

pect the person ahead to keep moving. So when Uncle
Elmer stopped sudden-like, I ran into him, whugg!
My face hit his back so hard that for a minute I
thought I was going to be eating fresh meat. My
head hit his shoulder with an awful jar that gave me
crazy dancing shapes before my eyes.

Then I saw why Uncle Elmer had stopped so fast.
Standing beside Henrietta were three teen-age boys.
Did I say standing? Attacking would be a better word
for what they were doing. There was a greasy-haired
blond kid with more freckles per square inch on his
face than I've ever seen. He was jumping on the
running board, making Henrietta rock like a ship with
galloping consumption. A sour-looking fellow with
long black hair and the shadow of a beard was kicking
the tires. I don't know why people tend to kick tires.
What do they expect to learn? And at the rear of the
car was a fat boy with a crew cut. He had the trunk
open and was pawing through our picnic supplies. He
was having a hard time because the car was rocking
so hard, but he didn't seem to be a bit discouraged.

The way they were acting really made me boil. I
was ready to take off and take them all on. Every one
of them. But Uncle Elmer stuck his arms out flat, like
a policeman holding back a crowd. I got the message.
And waited.

"Hey, Blimp," called the bearded one, who had
moved over to look in the front window. "Pipe the
dash panel. Man, it looks like a computer board. More
punch and push than a slot machine."

I knew Blimp had to be the fat one. Sure enough, he was the one who answered. "Okay, Zingo." (Now there was a nickname. Yet, I had to admit, it sort of fitted.) "I've gotta get the trunk lid down. Don't want to be a naughty Goldilocks and leave the Three Bears' house in a mess."

This remark seemed to strike the blond fellow as terribly funny. He stopped his jumping and laughed up a storm. "You're a pistol, Blimp . . . a regular pistol."

He hopped off the running board and pulled open the door on his side to get a better look at the dashboard. Zingo was climbing in behind the steering wheel. He closed the door on that side, but Freckles sort of lounged half in and half out of the car. They were both staring at that panel, kind of mesmerized. Well, that's the way it looked from where we were watching. But they weren't staring at all. They were looking for the ignition. And they found it too. Now wouldn't you think an old gal as smart as Henrietta wouldn't start for three such slobs?

But no! that engine roared into sound like a fire truck responding to a three alarmer. I had to shake my head at Henrietta's stupidity. We were all watching the boys so hard that we didn't see Petunia racing from the tall grass towards that open door. Blast that cat! he'd probably been there all the time that we were out beating the brush. And he wasn't about to be left.

He flew through the open door on Freckles's side

with all the daintiness of a pile driver. And since Petunia usually landed with claws extended I could guess how Freckles felt when Petunia zeroed in on his knee. He let out this yelp and flung Petunia off his leg. The action surprised Petunia. He launched an attack of his own. First he caught Freckles on the ankle with his wooden leg — rat-atat-tat. Then he made a slashing leap for the face. Naturally, Freckles grabbed to protect himself. But he had his eyes shut to protect them from Petunia's claws so he missed the cat and grabbed a handful of buttons on the panel.

And oh, what action he got then! The back of the front seat went down with a crash. Both boys went with it. Zingo's foot caught the panel, and whoosh! the back of the seat flipped them against the dashboard. Pushing themselves away, they hit the buttons, and whambo! they flipped over again.

"Hey, man! what action," said Blimp, looking in the window on Zingo's side. He started around the front of the car and as he passed the radiator, the cap flew off and a stream of water caught him smack on the side of the head. He gasped, wiping at the water which kept on coming. After he made his way through it, he wiped his eyes on his sleeve trying to clear his vision. So, of course, he didn't see the sides of the car coming down. I mean, who would expect that? He got caught by the top corner and down he went — side and boy together. Petunia by then had had enough of the ups and downs and shrieks so he took off over Freckles, using the dashboard as a spring.

And that added a bit more action. The car seats started vibrating. They shook and shimmied. In fact they shook so hard that the boys were shaken out of the car and onto the ground. There they lay. One on each side and, of course, one under the side. And a moment later the horn began honking — raucously and off key — "Hail, hail, the gang's all here." Out in the brush we found ourselves sitting on the ground. It was a necessity. We were all laughing so hard we couldn't stand up. But the boys weren't finding it so funny. Freckles and Zingo got to their feet and started toward the brown-orange sports car sitting at the side road.

"Blimp . . ." Zingo had to shout to be heard over the horn. "Where's Blimp?"

"The monster got him," said Freckles. His voice squeaked like a violin playing in the top range.

"Come on, man. To the rescue," shouted Zingo. They raced back to Henrietta, still gaily bouncing and booming out, "Hail, hail, the gang's all here." Freckles held up the side and Zingo pulled Blimp out. They sort of hoisted him to his feet, and with an arm over each shoulder they managed to stagger to the car. There they dumped Blimp head down, feet up, into the small back seat. Zingo jumped in the driver's seat and Freckles climbed in the other and they took off from that spot like they had TNT in their gas tank. But I noticed that as they were zooming away, Freckles had turned back toward Henrietta and was shaking his fist at her.

The rest of us left in the spot were shaking too. From laughter. Pufferdink's law had sure produced a dilly for us this time. I'd never seen anybody enjoy the unexpected as the five of us had. Though I don't think those three boys would have agreed that "enjoyment" was the right word. Anyway, once we'd calmed down, we had to go to work. Because the sides had to be put up again, and the radiator filled with water. We discovered that the thermos was almost empty and Uncle Elmer promised he'd stop at the first service station and get us some. Then we had to get Petunia corralled. That cat wanted nothing to do with humans or Henrietta which made it all pretty tough. But he finally relented and let us catch him.

We climbed in the back seat and were ready to go. Uncle Elmer shifted his long length around a bit, to find a comfortable position for driving. "I just hope, Elmer," said Aunt Em, "that Henrietta doesn't go around treating all strangers like that. She could get us in a peck of trouble. Which she may have done already." Aunt Em pulled the knitting needles out of the bun at the back of her head and began knitting.

"Don't borrow trouble, Em," said Uncle Elmer. "Dust my dandruff! It sure is rough on a man with two old women to please."

Aunt Em snorted. And Henrietta roared into sound and then died away. Uncle Elmer didn't seem to be paying any attention to either of them. He pushed the starter with his foot again. "Those boys deserved everything they got. And I, for one, am glad they got it."

Henrietta's engine roared into sound again and it had such a jaunty, throaty sound, that for just a minute there I thought she was saying, "Me too!" I was almost worried that Henrietta was taking such an interest in Pufferdink affairs. And then I thought of the expressions on those fellows' faces. And I forgot everything else.

ONCE under way on the highway we all got hit with
the most awful hunger. After all, a lot had happened
since breakfast, and what with the hunt for Petunia
and the excitement with the boys, we had had lots of
exercise. Uncle Elmer didn't even protest when
Aunt Em said she thought we ought to eat. He just
turned off into the first side road — to hunt for some
shade was what he said. And what a hunt we had. Because shade just doesn't come easy in that country.
Finally, way, way down this road he found a bluff.
So he pulled Henrietta right under it and we climbed
out to have a look at where we were. It looked like the
end of the earth, and a worn-out earth at that. Even
the brush had that dried, desperate quality of things
that never get enough water. Just the sight of it made
us all thirsty. Jenny begged for a drink and Aunt Em
said in a very tired way, "No, Jenny. Help with lunch
first." So Jenny did.

The heat seemed to be making us all drowsy. I
guess the events of the trip were beginning to tell on
our nervous systems. I know I felt absolutely pooped.
And I could tell Aunt Em must be feeling the same
way because she didn't seem to give a hoot whether
the lunch was nutritionally balanced or not. She said it
was too hot to cook and to make ourselves peanut butter sandwiches and open a bottle of pop apiece. At

the last minute she dug out a bottle of dill pickles and they seemed to help the sticky peanut butter slide down. Lately we'd been eating so many peanut butter sandwiches that every now and then I checked my fingers to see if they were beginning to get a shape like a peanut's.

Uncle Elmer yawned a couple of times while he was eating. Then he sort of stretched and suggested to Aunt Em that we might rest a bit before driving on to Rapid City — it wasn't far, he said. It sounded like a great idea to every one of us. We plunked down the air-mattresses wherever there was a spot of shade. And presto . . . we were gone. Bugs, snakes, dust — nothing stopped us from sleeping. Even Aunt Em. For once her hands were still. She had quit knitting.

I don't know how long we had slept. But when I came to, I could tell from the faded feel of the sun that it was getting toward late afternoon. There was a cool breeze rising off the prairie. And I felt refreshed. I stretched a bit, then got up on my elbow and found myself staring right into Pete's eyes. He was up on his knees looking at me.

"Hey, Chris," he whispered, "let's go exploring."

"Oh, no, you don't, young man," said Uncle Elmer. Obviously Pete's whisper had carried farther than he intended. "This is the kind of country where you stick together because you could get lost. Besides, it's time to move on. You two can help me pack the picnic stuff away. Jenny and Aunt Em can roll up the air-mattresses. Let's go. We need to find a camping spot for tonight."

We all did as we were told. Morning seemed eons of light years away. But we had a strangely peaceful feeling. Jenny swept Petunia up into her arms and climbed into Henrietta. It took only a few minutes to get everything ship shape. Then we followed her lead. Uncle Elmer started the engine and we jounced onto the dusty old road, headed, we hoped, toward the highway. Into the quiet Uncle Elmer suddenly boomed out in his singing, off-key voice. Well, it wasn't exactly that it was off key so much as that he kept changing keys as he was singing which certainly made for a different sound. Nobody else sang. We were satisfied to just sit and listen to the spirit and the sounds.

And then it happened. This skunk — well, it looked like a skunk, ambled right in front of our wheels. Henrietta zigged. She zagged. And that's quite an adventure on a narrow road. Suddenly we weren't on the road, because while we were zagging or zigging a bang shook the whole car. Away we went across country. Right in front of us was a barbed-wire fence. But did that stop us? I should say not. With twanging, twunging sounds we burst through and away. Below us, near a tank (that's what farmers call them, though they still look like ponds to me) there was a whole group of cattle. Down the hill charged Henrietta, right at those animals and the water. For a minute

I thought we might have steak for dinner. But the cattle scattered, which was a more sensible action than I had really expected. Uncle Elmer was braking like mad, but we skidded and slewed in the mud. Then about twenty feet from the edge of the water, we came to a stop. And we sat there, dazed, looking around.

"What," said Aunt Em, "was that all about?"

"I think it was a skunk, Aunt Em," said Jenny. "'Cause it smelled like a skunk and looked like a skunk."

"Whooee!" said Uncle Elmer. "I'll say it was a skunk. A skunk and a blowout. So now we're in trouble."

"Well, Elmer," said Aunt Em, "trouble's getting to be such a natural condition for us on this trip, that I don't feel comfortable unless we're right up to our ears in it."

"What kind of trouble are we in, Uncle Elmer?" asked Pete. Pete was the practical one. He liked to know exactly what he was facing.

"It's like this, Pete. You know we had that flat yesterday out in the badlands?"

"Yep."

"And you remember how crowded this morning was with activity what with your having to get gas and then our buying food and visiting the drug store and the run-in with the boys?"

"Yep."

"Well, you see, we plain forgot to have the spare

patched. So here we are out in the middle of nowhere
with two bum tires. Now what do you think of that?"

"I for one think it's pretty poor planning," said
Aunt Em. "But as long as we're here, we might as well
enjoy it. Let's say that Henrietta has picked our camp
site for us. We've got water and company" (at this she
kind of sneered in the direction of the cattle, which
made Pete and me snicker) "and we've got privacy."

"Right as usual, Em. Pufferdink's law is operating
again."

"Enjoy the unexpected," we chanted.

"That's right," said Uncle Elmer. So we piled out of
the car.

Pete had the brilliant idea that we should all go for
a swim. But Uncle Elmer squashed the idea in about
two seconds flat. He said a loud, flat NO. Then he explained so that Pete could understand. And Pete did
understand with the thinking side of his brain that
unknown water could be tricky, that the bottom was
messy and that it was probably awfully dirty, what
with animals tramping about in it. Uncle Elmer also
added that neither he nor Aunt Em could swim so if
we got in trouble it would be "goodbye Nelson kids."
But Pete's unthinking side kept wishing he could go
swimming.

We did feel hot. And we got feeling hotter. First
Pete and I got out the gasoline stove and started it for
Aunt Em, because she thought we should have a hot
meal. Then we helped Uncle Elmer with the tire,

patching it as best we could. And we'd hardly finished that when Uncle Elmer suggested we should go up and fix the fence where we'd burst through it. Only we didn't get that done right then, because Aunt Em was demanding that we bring over the groceries. As soon as I lifted that thermos of water, I knew we were in trouble. So much had happened that nobody had thought about stopping at a service station for more water. And it was certain sure that there wasn't anything drinkable very close at hand. Well, when Aunt Em found the state of the water jug she was fit to be tied. She started out talking and the words came like a torrent. We were almost drowned in words. Not that it helped our situation a mite, except maybe to let off steam for Aunt Em.

Then Uncle Elmer came up with a corking idea. "Em . . . Now, Em . . . Calm down a bit. We don't have water but we do have scads of pop."

"Pop? I can imagine what a great and tremendous help that will be. What are you suggesting I should do with pop?" She folded her arms and glared at him. I was surprised that he had the courage to go on. Aunt Em looked that fierce.

"I was thinking, Em, that I've never tasted green beans in lime pop nor potatoes boiled in grape. Now there's an idea worth trying. Necessity's the mother of invention, they say."

"Hey," I suddenly shouted. "Hey, I remember reading a story about a baby sitter who cooked food in pop. And those kids thought it was great."

"I remember that too," said Pete. "Can we try it, Aunt Em? Please?"

"We'll see. We'll see," said Aunt Em. "This trip gets nuttier all the time. Cooking in pop, yet." But you could tell by the tone of her voice that she was weakening. What a meal . . . what a meal that was. Aunt Em had cooked the frozen beans in lime pop and the potatoes in grape — the bologna she cooked in orange. And she washed the lettuce in grape pop, which gave the salad a nice flavor. I tell you, there was a new taste treat. Simply wonderful. I bet even a French chef couldn't produce the equal of that meal.

We ate until Pete's stomach got that round tight look a stomach gets when it's packed to capacity. And he had this happy, foolish look on his face. Jenny was often pretty finicky about her food but this evening she tried everything and kept right on trying. Even Aunt Em wasn't too critical. She did remark that the potatoes were a bit purple for her taste and that was all.

We took our time about eating. But it came — as it always does come — the moment when the good food is gone and the dishwashing must begin. Unfortunately we had run out of paper plates, so tonight for the first time we had used Aunt Em's heavy crockery picnic plates. And I'm not kidding when I say they were heavy. A stack of them almost made me stagger. We couldn't throw these away. So, dishwashing was inevitable.

"Well, Elmer. I see the moment of truth is at hand."

Aunt Em was always saying crazy things like that. "Could be, Em. Supposin' you tell me what truth you're speaking of?"

"You've been bragging about how wonderful Henrietta is. And I admit that some of your bragging has proved pretty accurate. Now I'm waiting to see how you plan for that ugly hunk of metal to wash the dishes." She looked at Uncle Elmer with doubt written all over her face.

"Oh, that, Em. Why, that's no problem at all. For a moment there you had me scared. But washing dishes? Shucks, that's simple for Henrietta. Come lend a hand, children."

I'd rather do most anything than wash dishes so I lent a very eager hand. So did Pete. Aunt Em corralled Jenny to help scrape the dishes and put away the food.

First Uncle Elmer rummaged through the stuff in the luggage carrier and came up with a round, platter-like thing. Reminded me of the turntable for a phonograph. And the more I looked at it the more certain I was that it probably had been just that at some time. He started to fiddle with the platter and the right front fender, telling Pete and me at the same time to hunt up a big kettle on top of the car. We felt and fumbled through lumps and humps and finally came up with this big old pot.

All the time it was getting dusk around us. We hadn't realized how late it really was. Good times never seem to last long enough. And that's a strange and very real fact. We hauled the kettle over to Aunt

Em, and galloping goose-eggs! when we took off the top, it was lined with racks to hold dishes just like a regular dishwasher. Even Aunt Em admitted that she was a mite surprised. But we didn't have time to enjoy our surprise long, because Aunt Em handed Pete and me two buckets and told us to go down to the pond and fill them full. She said to hurry because the water had to boil for twenty minutes to purify it.

Pete and I got to the water's edge safe enough. Some of the cattle acted a little funny, as if they wondered what we were doing there. Pete waded into the water and got one bucket full, which he then handed to me. I started up the incline with it. And then behind me I heard this splash. Pete, of course. I knew he'd figure out a way to get in that water. He paddled around a bit, grinning from ear to ear. Then in a minute, he scooped up another bucket of water and came dripping along behind me.

Aunt Em looked at him sort of fierce when he handed her the water, but she didn't say a word. She just put the water on to boil. And Pete and I went back to watching Uncle Elmer. He had the turntable fastened on the fender all right, and he was busy looping a long rubber belt, like a fan belt, underneath it. Then he hooked it up where the regular fan belt ran. "Turn on the engine, Pete," said Uncle Elmer, "let's see if she works."

Of course, it did. When Pete pushed the purple button with D marked on it, the turntable started to spin around. Round and round it went. I kept watching and as I watched I wondered . . . if the kettle spun like that what would happen to the dishes? Aunt Em must have had the same identical thought. "Mercy on us, Elmer, you aren't planning on whirling the dishes on that spinning saucer?"

"Nope, Em, not exactly. I plan to whirl the kettle which will spin the water which will wash the dishes. Good thinking, eh?"

"Crazy thinking to my mind," said Aunt Em. "I don't think, Elmer, that you realize that those dishes will break. And I can't think of anything that Henrietta would enjoy more than breaking up my crockery."

"Now Em, that's no way to talk about Henrietta after all she's done for this family. If you've got the dishes and water ready, we can go ahead."

It took both Pete and me to carry the kettle loaded with dishes over to Uncle Elmer. We plunked it down on the turntable. Whoee! it was heavy. Then Uncle Elmer put in some soap powder, poured over a bucket of boiled water, fastened down the lid and told Pete to start the engine. Which he did. Then Pete pushed the purple button and the turntable began to turn — slowly, slowly at first. Then faster and faster. Pete discovered that the harder he pushed on the accelerator the faster it spun. Aunt Em started yelling about her dishes, and Uncle Elmer was shouting to Pete to let the engine idle and Henrietta was roaring up a storm. For a moment there it was pretty noisy. Pete finally got the message and let Henrietta run the dishwasher without extra push from him. I could hear the water swishing inside the kettle and although I listened hard I couldn't hear any dishes breaking. Uncle Elmer said we should let them wash for fifteen minutes, so Jenny and I packed away the gasoline stove and the odds and ends from the supper. It was pretty dark by now and the moon was beginning to rise. So, of course, Henrietta was beginning to glow.

Earlier Jenny and Pete had scrounged around to find little pieces of wood for a fire. After their long search we knew why the pioneers had burned buffalo chips. There sure wasn't much wood around. Still, we had enough for a very little fire. Aunt Em pulled her rocker up close to the spot and we watched while the tiny flame flickered, then took hold and began to burn. Even these few flames cast a nice comforting glow. You have no idea how lonely the outdoors can seem until you're out in a big empty space by yourself. Especially when way off in the distance some strange animal howls.

"What's that?" asked Jenny, moving just a little closer to Aunt Em.

"H'mm, sounds like old Mr. Coyote talking to the moon," said Uncle Elmer.

"But why do they want to talk to the moon?" asked Jenny.

"Because coyotes have been talking to the moon since the day the Lord created them," said Uncle Elmer. "Since this is sure 'nuff coyote country, you're going to have to get used to hearing them talk."

And right then we heard another howl. And from

way in the distance a mournful answer. It made little prickles start right up from my ankles until I could feel my goose pimples having goose pimples. Jenny and I moved closer to the fire and closer to each other. Seemed to me that Aunt Em pulled her rocker in closer to the bit of flame too.

"It's eerie, that's what it is. Has an unnatural sound," said Aunt Em. "I keep wishing they'd stop."

"They won't, Em, and that's the way it is. Say, Chris, get the other pot of water. I think we're ready for the rinsing."

Uncle Elmer walked over to the car and shouted to Pete to stop the engine. Then he screwed a cap off the bottom of the kettle and the soapy water ran out, with gushing enthusiasm. Of course, you know the next step in the plan. We had to pour the clean water in at the top. We got the kettle locked up again and Pete started it whirling. I don't know quite why, but I felt safer somehow, standing near Henrietta. Maybe because of her funny glow. Maybe just because she was the biggest thing around. We could hear the cattle moving and stomping and shifting, but they gave us a comfortable feeling of having company. Which helped.

And then out of the dark and right on top of a coyote's long-drawn-out howl, came a gruff voice. "Put your hands up!!"

Of course, we did. We couldn't see a thing and the voice sounded like it wanted no nonsense. But you feel mighty silly standing out in the middle of nowhere with your hands in the air. Two lumpy shapes moved out of the shadows towards us. We could see a reflection of our tiny fire on something metal. It looked like a rifle . . . or maybe a revolver. Anyway, for certain sure those men were armed and mean looking. Which was even more frightening. Aunt Em stood up. Sitting in a rocker holding knitting and needles over her head was rather awkward. Well, when she stood up she stepped on Petunia's tail. As I've said, that cat never let anyone make a mistake like that without knowing it. He turned with a slashing motion at Aunt Em, but managed to catch Jenny with the extended claw. Which caused Jenny to jump. She kicked the little bits of burning wood and one chunk flew into the air. I guess it landed on Petunia's back, because that cat let out this unearthly howl and was off and running. Now all this action and screeching had unnerved those men, I'm sure. And they weren't prepared for Petunia's rushing by them. He clunked one of the men on the ankle with his wooden leg. The man yelled out, grabbed for the rushing form and his gun went off.

Whambo, a bullet sizzled right at Uncle Elmer and me. First thing we knew was when we heard this pinging sound as metal met metal. Henrietta had been hit. Believe me, Uncle Henry and I didn't stand on any ceremony. We dropped to the ground and got as flat as we could. And then the action really began.

Because that bullet had nicked the latch on the whirling dishwasher. Pete was bouncing about in the car shouting about bandits and guns and watch out. And as he yelled he stomped on the accelerator which made the kettle whirl faster and faster. Next the lid whirled off like a platter from outer space in a hurry to get somewhere. But that wasn't all that went whirling. The dishes started flying like a whole squadron of flying saucers. I heard the men shouting. "Down . . . down, Jack." "My gosh! they're attacking." "Watch it!"

And I must say this last direction was a sensible one because there was plenty to watch. What a display. Dish after dish went zooming right at those men. But instead of hitting the ground in a sensible fashion, the men started to run. A dinner plate caught one on the rump. A cup banged the second on the head. Then a bowl got the first one in the shoulder blades and saucers and plastic glasses beat a tattoo on the other's back. They were almost out of range, when Pete hit the accelerator even harder. And whoosh! out came the big platter traveling rapidly. We could hear the dull thump as the second fellow got caught smack on the head. His rifle made an arc into the air and he went down like a felled tree. His friend ran back to him, bent over the figure and tried to drag him to his feet. Next thing we knew, there was Jenny standing with this long rifle in her hands. The barrel was weaving up and down . . . she was so scared. But she had it aimed in the right direction. Right towards those fellows. And she said the right words. Well, at least the ones they're always saying in TV dramas. "You drop your gun, or I'll shoot."

The unhurt man sized up his danger mighty quickly, because plunk! there was his gun on the ground. But Uncle Elmer was almost faster. He covered that ground between Henrietta and Jenny in record time and he had to start from a stomach position. He grabbed the rifle.

"Dust my duds! gal . . . that was quick thinking. But you're a mite small for this size fire-arm. Now let's find out what those men want."

Which was, of course, what we all wanted to know. Were they bandits or maniacs or . . . ? That question mark opened lots of possibilities. Well, Aunt Em rushed over to see if she could help with the unconscious man — Henrietta packs a mean wallop. She sent Pete and me for buckets of water and that Pete! he gets carried away with the helping spirit. He poured so much water on the poor guy, that he almost drowned him. Still, the man did revive pretty quickly. It was either that or strangle.

After things had calmed down a bit, we found out that the two men weren't bad men at all. As I said to Pete, too bad they hadn't worn white hats, because on TV the good men always wear white hats. Seems that the break in the fence had been found by a rancher who had notified the owner and the sheriff. So the two men had come looking, expecting rustlers at least. When they spotted the glowing car and heard the rackety-rack noise of the dishwasher, they thought we'd set up a branding station to change brands on the cattle.

Man, how we laughed. The thought of Aunt Em or Jenny as rustlers struck all of us funny. Even the sheriff managed a weak laugh. The owner had too sore a head to manage anything more than a weak smile. 'Course, right away he wanted to know how we had thrown all those flying missiles at them. They couldn't believe the dishwasher set up on Henrietta. But then, I suppose most people wouldn't believe Henrietta at all. She's that remarkable.

In spite of all their lumps and bumps from the flying crockery, Mr. Cory, the rancher, and Mr. Mulford, the sheriff, were awfully good sports. They had a bottle of warm pop with us and then Mr. Cory offered to pull Henrietta into town with his pick-up so that we could get the tires expertly patched. The sheriff said he'd lead the way and we kids could ride with him. Uncle Elmer promised Aunt Em that he'd bring her back early the next morning to hunt for her dishes so she agreed to leave.

Can you guess what happened next? 'Course, we told the sheriff about the boys and how Henrietta had shaken them up in order to escape their mauling and how we had almost landed in the lake because of the blowout. We even told him how Henrietta had saved Petunia when he fell in the lake. Well, Mr. Mulford thought it was a mighty remarkable story and that Henrietta was mighty remarkable herself . . . in fact so remarkable that she was almost unbelievable. Then he suggested that maybe we ought to celebrate the slam-bang ending to our day. So he turned on his siren. And with that sound howling and whining over our heads we sailed into town. Pufferdink's law. Enjoy the unexpected. And jumping jelly beans! with Henrietta along, we always had lots of unexpected things to enjoy.

A Day of Springs

AFTER all the excitement we had had, sightseeing was a nice change. We finally made it into the Black Hills. We saw Mt. Rushmore — now there's a fantastic piece of manmade sculpture. 'Course, we had to hang onto Pete, who was determined to go and crawl down Washington's nose. But we finally convinced him that the men up there were workmen, not visitors. He gave up pretty reluctantly. And we saw Custer State Park, and Lead and Deadwood and the Homestead Gold Mine and even got out to see the piece of carving on the mountain of the Indian chief, Crazy Horse. Finally we decided to spend the last days of our holiday in the camp ground at Sylvan Lake.

Henrietta was a real curiosity piece to the rest of the campers. The first night she washed the dishes, half the camp gathered round. And the sleeping arrangements caused another furor. But then people got used to the "differentness" of both Henrietta and the Pufferdinks. After all, an old lady madly knitting at a long red tube for a giraffe's neck can cause quite a stir too. But being considered "different" didn't seem to bother Aunt Em much. I guess she'd been different so long that she hardly noticed it. I have to admit that it still made me get uneasy twinges in my stomach to find people looking sideways at me, but maybe I'll get

over it. I guess I'll have to if I'm going to travel with
Aunt Em and Uncle Elmer.

On our third day in camp Uncle Elmer sort of eased
into an idea that he'd been thinking over. "How about
climbing Mt. Harney?" he asked.

"Oh, let's! Please let's," said Jenny. She was talking, not to Uncle Elmer, but to Aunt Em, who had this
determined set look to her face.

"Now, Elmer Pufferdink," said Aunt Em. "That's
unfair. You know I hate hiking. It's dull . . . it's
work. Knitting . . . that's my speed. And then you
suggest mountain climbing?"

"Yep, but not the kind of mountain climbing where
you go up with axes and pitons and fingernails." Uncle
Elmer didn't finish.

"Oh, boy, Uncle Elmer! Let's go . . . when do we
start?" That was me interrupting. I'd been thinking so
hard about mountain climbing that I didn't hear him
say it wasn't the exciting kind. So of course, I felt disappointed when his words finally percolated through
to my brain. Seems he was suggesting we walk to the
top of Mt. Harney. I'm afraid I agreed with Aunt Em.
Walking is work, and walking uphill is murder. But as
Uncle Elmer described the ranger station at the top
and how we could see the whole area — miles and
miles laid out before us — I decided it was worth it.
So you see, he had no trouble at all selling us kids the
idea. But Aunt Em? There was a different situation.

She set her chin firmly in that way people do when
they've made up their minds. And she'd made up her

mind all right. Not to go. But that Uncle Elmer, I tell you, he always had some crazy and wonderful idea.

"Em, if I made the walking easy, would you go?"

"Humph," said Aunt Em, "I'd like to see what could do that. Wings maybe?"

"No, springs," said Uncle Elmer. "You'll see. I've been working at the idea for some time. Even tried it at home. And it works. Never fear, Em."

"If Henrietta has anything to do with it, I'll be scared plumb silly," said Aunt Em.

"Not exactly, though I'll have to call on her for a little help," said Uncle Elmer. Which left us all guessing what he meant. But not for long. He got Pete and me to haul out the back seat. Then he upended it and pulled out two big springs — gigantic ones.

"You're hurting Henrietta," said Jenny in a worried way.

"Dust my duds, gal! Henrietta's glad to help. We'll put them back as good as new when we're through using them." While he was talking he screwed on two metal plates, one on each spring. Then he threaded some leather straps through holes in the metal plates and one end of the strap was fitted with a buckle. When he had finished he held them up for us to see. "What do you think of those?"

"Hey . . . hey!" shouted Pete.

"Jumpers," said Jenny.

"Suicide weapons," said Aunt Em in a dry way. "You don't actually expect me to use those, Elmer?"

"Em, I tell you, it's like flying. Try them on . . . go

on, try them." He was urging her with such enthusi-
asm, that for a minute I thought he had her convinced.
But Aunt Em was pretty slow to shift her opinion.
"Un-uh. Let's see one of the children use them first.
I've got this funny feeling that one second after I had
them on, I'd be stretched out flat on the ground.
Powee!"

Jenny, being the youngest, got the first chance. Now
there's a funny thing. On fun things, they give the
youngest first try. But if it's a work thing, they let the
oldest have first try. On the other hand, old Pete
there usually got second chance at everything. I
couldn't decide if this made the middle position better
or worse. But I didn't spend much time thinking about
it. Instead I turned to watch Jenny. It was like seeing
a kangaroo with pigtails. Each leap carried her farther
and farther until some of her bounces were taking her
twenty feet at a time. 'Course, right away everybody
in the camp ground started to gather. We were lucky
that most of them were off sight-seeing or it would
have been a mob. But then, I suppose seeing someone
taking gigantic leaps through the air is a somewhat un-
usual sight. Pete got his chance at the jumpers and I
had a fling at it too. It was like flying. Earthbound
flying. Things went by in a blur, but all the sounds and
colors and smells blended together to give you a feeling of joy like your heart was going to lift you right
over into the clouds. And you were free. Really free.

When I bounded back to the family, all the camp
kids were clamoring for a turn. Uncle Elmer was po-

lite but very firm. He said, No, we were due to leave, that he couldn't let one do it and not another, but when we got back, he'd see they had a turn.

They were pretty disappointed, but it was a fair proposition, so one by one they disappeared. Aunt Em kept sitting in her rocker. She seemed to be rocking and knitting and frowning in rhythm. Then she stopped and looked fiercely at us. My heart went "Thump!" like it was made of lead. And then she said, "All right. All right. I can tell you've made up your minds that I have to go. Mercy on us! why I have to trail along is beyond me. But if it makes you happy, I'll give the springers a try. Only you go first.

I don't aim to do my practice and cavorting in front of an audience. Besides, looks to me as if they're pretty speedy. So have no fear, I'll catch up." And she was so right.

Uncle Elmer told Aunt Em how to find the trail and then he led the rest of us off, like a general leading his troops. Or does a general go in the rear? I'm not sure, but he was for certain sure leading us and at a fearsome clip. Those long limbs of his stretched out and made the rest of us double-time. I glanced back as we were going out of sight, and there was Aunt Em, rocking and rocking, and petting Petunia, who was lying in her lap.

We had been hiking along, at least thirty minutes, and the trail had that wonderful smell of the mountains — one part pine, one part sharp air, and one part blooming wild flowers. It smelled so good you wished you could bottle it for some depressing, gray day in the winter. So we were moving along, slower now, smelling the smells and each thinking his own thoughts, when we heard this racket behind us. A twanging and a shouting and a thudding. "Elllmer . . . Elllmer." There was a pause.

"Here, Em, here we are." 'Course, we weren't sure where we were, but that's what people always shout anyway.

"Stop   me . . . Stop   me.   No   brakes!!!!   No brakes . . . !" And Aunt Em's words had barely reached us when she was there too, bounding forward like an express train. She held her feet together and jumped. But wow! what distances she covered. Seemed as if each jump took her higher and farther. The knitting needles in her hair were vibrating like a nervous caterpillar's antennae and hanging over her shoulder . . . jumping jelly beans! Aunt Em had Petunia in the knitting bag slung on her back. That cat was clinging to her shoulder as if he were glued with epoxy cement.

Well, it's a strange and very real fact, that when you're startled you tend to freeze. Your brain stops ordering your body to move. So when Aunt Em came roaring up the trail like that, we simply stood and gawked. We didn't move a muscle except maybe our eye muscles as we followed her action and our mouth muscles as they dropped open in surprise. Whoosh! Aunt Em was past, just like that. And then we moved. Too late to really do anything, but all of us started running up that trail. We could hear her twanging and hollering and getting farther away. And then came a sound that made my eyes bug out. It was that terrible shriek Aunt Em had let loose with when she thought she saw the rattlesnake.

I couldn't swallow. Suddenly, my throat felt tight. We kept wondering and running. Oh, we were scared all right. And ahead of us, coming closer, we heard this thumping, pounding sound, very heavy. Mixed in with it were growling noises which surely couldn't be Petunia. "Em, Em? Where are you?" shouted Uncle Elmer. He could barely get it out, because he was gasping so hard from running up-hill.

"Merciful heavens, I'm bareback." Her tone was half wail, half astonishment.

We hardly had time to figure out how Aunt Em had found a horse when this thing, this shaggy, brown, mammoth animal, came round the bend. We jumped. It was jump or be run over. And my gollee! Aunt Em was sitting on the rump of a huge brown bear, riding backwards and clutching him for dear life. And Petunia was clutching her. And that poor bear looked so scared that he needed someone to clutch too. Only I didn't want it to be me he clutched.

"Do something," shrieked Aunt Em at Uncle Elmer, who was so stunned that he couldn't move. I mean, Aunt Em riding a bear was something to see. And then as if this order had inspired her to action, Aunt Em grabbed a knitting needle from her hair and jabbed that bear in the rump with all the strength she could muster. Which was quite a bit I guess, considering the bear's reaction. That poor critter let out an unearthly shriek and tore off the path and into the brush, trying to knock Aunt Em off. Only he hadn't reckoned with Aunt Em. Our last view was of Aunt Em crouching low and striking that bear again and again. And Petunia was hissing and spitting in her ear. He was sure giving her moral support if nothing else.

We started running again, only we had to reverse our direction in order to keep after Aunt Em. Suddenly we realized that all the shrieking, howling and growling had stopped. It was hard going through that brush, even though the bear had made quite a path. Since the trail up the mountain was a series of switchbacks, it took us only a moment in the brambles and pines to reach the next piece of trail. Once there we couldn't believe our eyes. There was the bear, lying limp and inert on the path, his head resting against a boulder. We found Petunia mighty fast because of his hideous, mournful meowing above our heads. He was right smack near the top of a pine tree. Whatever blow had stopped the bear, had catapulted Petunia into the tree. And the limb he was perched on looked mighty fragile. No wonder he was crying.

But Aunt Em? we couldn't see her. Then we heard her voice and another voice too, a rather deep, male voice. They were coming down the trail from above us. And then, there were Aunt Em and a Ranger. The Ranger was red-haired, fresh-faced (well, aren't they always?) and big. He looked like a character right out of a Canadian movie about the Royal Mounted Police. But he looked mad too and, if possible, Aunt Em looked still madder. He had a firm grip on her arm so she bounced along beside him with only little leaps.

"Do you know this woman, sir?" he asked Uncle Elmer.

"Yes siree, that's my wife, Emma Pufferdink. I'm Elmer Pufferdink."

And he held out his hand to the Ranger, who being polite let go of Aunt Em to shake Uncle Elmer's hand. Well, that sent Aunt Em off down the trail on those

leaping springers. Only this time, Pete and I both reached out and grabbed her as she went past.

"Take me to that tree. Take me to that tree," she said.

I don't know why that remark struck me so funny. It reminded me of a Martian ordering people to take him to their leader. Anyway, both Pete and I snickered, though maybe we weren't snickering at the same thing, and we helped Aunt Em over to a tall old pine that had a nice bare trunk. She held on to it as if she were drowning.

Behind us, the Ranger was introducing himself to Uncle Elmer as men will do. He said his name was Angus McFarland, that he was coming off duty, and that meeting this lady had absolutely bowled him over.

We could believe it. Can't you see Aunt Em and Angus going head over heels when they collided? After all, on a quiet Wednesday afternoon in the mountains, who would expect someone to come leaping up the trail on auto springs? He'd hardly finished remarking on meeting Aunt Em when he saw the bear. "Say, what happened here?" he asked.

I don't think he expected an answer. People usually don't when they ask a question like that. He was bending over the bear and listening, for a heart beat, I suppose, when Aunt Em said, "I was riding that silly animal."

"Riding the bear?" Angus McFarland's face was the funniest mixture of expressions. His brain was signaling his face all right, but it kept shifting the signals. So he looked surprised, and horrified and angry and amused in just that order. "You aren't supposed to ride the bears in the Black Hills, ma'am."

"Young man, I'll have you know it wasn't my idea. It was that fool animal's."

"You mean the bear, ma'am?" Angus looked as if he couldn't believe his ears.

"Of course, I mean the bear. You didn't think I meant the cat, did you?" And since Angus didn't know about the cat at all he looked still more baffled. "Oh, it's simple," said Aunt Em. "I was bouncing along the trail, springing's more like it, I guess, trying to catch up with the family. I'd discovered that the jumpers were a great idea except that I didn't have the foggiest idea of how to stop except by running into something. Well, Petunia was pretty scared. He was riding on my back, you see . . ."

"Petunia's the cat," said Jenny helpfully.

"Oh, of course . . . of course, the cat was on your back." The ranger looked like a person who has just stepped into a nightmare world where the unbelievable is believable.

"Yes, Petunia. I said that," said Aunt Em so crossly that she bounced a bit and had to get a firmer grip on the tree. "Well, I yelled at the family to stop me, but the durn fools let me bounce right by, though I could hear them running behind me. Then suddenly, smack in the path ahead was this bear. Now I yelled at him . . ."

"Shrieked's the word, Em," said Uncle Elmer.

"I let him know I was coming, but did he step aside? Oh, no. Not him. That fool bear backed up. There I was, already in the air in a mighty jump, planning to go right over him since he wouldn't move out of the way, and he went and backed up. And you know what happened then, don't you?"

"You landed right on the bear," shouted Pete, so excited that he couldn't help adding his bit.

"Right you are, Pete. On his back . . . only backwards. He was facing down trail and I was facing up trail and Petunia was hissing and spitting and giving me fits on the pack trail, so to speak. 'Course, that bear didn't take it calmly. He started down the path. There was no stopping him. I tried everything — kicking, pleading, yelling, reasoning, but he was off and running. Whoever said that bears weren't very smart said a mouthful. I yelled at the family that I was bear back and to stand away — which they did."

"Bareback?" said the Ranger.

"Naturally, bear back. What would you call it?" asked Aunt Em belligerently. "So when the bear wouldn't listen to reason, I took my knitting needle and whammed it right into his hide . . . wham! WHAM!"

She bounced dangerously high as she emphasized the whams. It took her a minute to get her bounces calmed down. "You struck that bear?" said the Ranger.

" 'Course, I struck him. Comes a time when a body

has to do something. I told you bears weren't too bright and this one sure proved it. There he was running forward, but trying to look backwards at me. Zoweee! he hit that boulder an awful smack. Petunia disappeared and I got thrown off, right on the jumpers which bounced me up-trail until you thoughtfully stopped me."

"I wouldn't say there was much thought involved," said the Ranger in sort of a dazed way.

"It sure shows you what comes of not looking," said Aunt Em.

"It does?" said Jenny.

"Sure thing," said Aunt Em. "If that bear had been tending to his looking, he'd still be running. Which I guess is lucky for me."

The Ranger kept shaking his head and looking first at Aunt Em and then at Uncle Elmer and then at us kids and back to the bear. I think he was almost ready to say something when a shape hurtled down towards us, from over our heads. We'd all been thinking and chuckling so hard at Aunt Em's story, that we'd forgotten Petunia. The limb must have given way, because here came cat and limb in a mighty fast descent.

The branch caught in the tree, but darned if that cat didn't land smack in the knitting bag. Whoeee! what a jar he got. And he hit so hard that he sent Aunt Em zooming into the air. But Pete and I were getting awfully fast on the draw. We grabbed Aunt Em on only the second bounce and held her until she was only vibrating a bit.

"This is fantastic . . . I mean, it's really unbelievable. Do you know who this bear is?"

"Merciful heavens," said Aunt Em, "don't tell me the bear was somebody we should know."

"Not exactly. But it is the rogue bear we've been chasing for weeks. He's been terrorizing the camp grounds. A regular mischief maker. Dangerous too. Can't say I'm sorry to see him dead."

"Dead?" We all said the word together. Somehow we'd never even thought of that possibility. I thought he was simply unconscious.

"Dead as a mackerel! So we'll have to have you fill out a few forms. I don't quite know how to tell the chief that the most dangerous animal in the park in decades got knocked off by a little old lady on bed springs. He'll never believe it."

I had to admit he had a problem. We left him standing beside the bear, shaking his head and muttering. We seemed automatically, without even consulting, to turn back downhill and towards the camp. After all how could any mere landscape compare with the picture of Aunt Em riding the bear? After her wild adventure, even mountain climbing seemed tame. So we called it a day.

THAT night was not a night like all nights. There was a feel of something very special in the air. Perhaps we were all a little worn out with the excitement of running into the bear. Or perhaps after something so way out, we enjoyed taking our time doing familiar routine things — you know, savoring the moment — almost as if we had to taste thoroughly of each simple thing because we might not be doing the same thing very soon again. There was a snap in the air, as if the mildness had vanished with the sun. And the smell? It was different and yet the same as it had been that afternoon. Perhaps the added whiff of wood smoke from the fires was making the difference.

Supper was very special. We had steak sandwiches and our favorite ranch style beans plus carrot sticks. Then Uncle Elmer helped Pete and me build a nice, roaring fire and we made s'mores. Aunt Em told us how to do it, while she sat in her rocker, knitting, knitting. First we took graham crackers and laid on some squares of Hershey Bar. Then each of us toasted a marshmallow, slapped it down on the chocolate and topped the whole thing with another graham cracker. Talk about heavenly food. Angels couldn't eat better.

And Jenny agreed. "Ummm-um, Aunt Em. These s'mores are good."

"Want s'more?" asked Aunt Em and she had just a

bit of a twinkle in her eye. Of course . . . that's how they got that crazy name.

"I bet," said Jenny, never tumbling, "that you're just about the best cook in the whole wide world, Aunt Em. Except for my mommy." She paused and in that pause it was strange, but I felt almost as if there were some warm presence around us — a soft cloud of love. I don't know if the sudden mention of our mother had suddenly made us aware of that wonderful enveloping love we had all lost or if it had always been there and we simply hadn't noticed. "Of course," said Jenny, "my mommy is dead."

She said it, right out like that. It was the first time that any of us had said out loud that our parents were dead. Somehow, we'd had the feeling that if we never spoke those words we could keep the fact from being true. But it's a strange and very real fact, that putting something in words tends to make it more real than just the thinking of it. I knew a great gulping rush of sadness for a moment and then it was gone. Jenny had said the words. And with the saying we all accepted the fact. Our folks were dead.

I had a feeling then of something ending. But what was ending? Perhaps I was crossing out of childhood, that marvelous world where nothing bad should ever happen. I suppose I had finally accepted that the wonderful life with our parents had ended and that another life was beginning. Or maybe it was because our adventures were coming to an end. The trip was almost over. Whatever it was, I knew I had a breathless, almost empty feeling that comes when one thing is ending and the next hasn't begun. I was hanging there in a vague emptiness, just wondering, when Aunt Em let out this funny sound. It really startled me because I was so far away in my thoughts. She sort of squeaked and crowed all at once. I felt a laugh bubbling from somewhere. It broke surface and we were all laughing. Aunt Em looked a little cross. Then she smiled her crooked, funny smile. "Merciful heavens!" she said, "I didn't expect you to burst out laughing just because I had finished. Look at it. The neck warmer is finished."

I told you something was ending. What a letdown. Aunt Em had finished the giraffe's neck warmer. She held one end aloft and it dropped away into a coil on the ground. The idea that my strange, dramatic feelings of something ending was only a forewarning of Aunt Em's reaching the end of her knitting project struck me so funny that I laughed again. And it's a strange and wonderful fact that if you start laughing, pretty soon people are laughing right with you. Even Aunt Em joined in. We were probably all laughing at different things, but it felt good. Just right for that moment.

Of course, next we stretched the neck warmer out full length, and it really stretched. It was the craziest looking red wool tube that you ever did see. It was fatter at one end than the other, just like a giraffe's neck. Oh, Aunt Em had thought of everything. Right now she was marching up and down the neck warmer's length looking carefully at each section to be sure there were no mistakes. Considering the strange and wild adventures that had been going on since she had started, I thought it mighty surprising that it could pass inspection. But Aunt Em gave a quick, satisfied nod at the end of her tour and said, "It looks fine to me. How about you, Elmer?"

"Couldn't be better, Em," said Uncle Elmer. He held his end real high as if he were sighting along it. "I tell you, Em, you're one fine knitter. This is a champion piece of knitting. What should we do with it?"

"Roll it up. Careful, now," said Aunt Em. "It can travel back home in the knitting bag. I'll mail it to the zoo from there."

Uncle Elmer did the rolling and the rest of us held up our piece of the neck warmer to keep it off the ground. With a satisfied pat, Uncle Elmer shoved the coil of wool into the knitting bag. And Aunt Em absent-mindedly stuck the knitting needles back in her bun. They had begun to look very natural there. When she came back from putting the knitting bag in the car, she was all business. And we found ourselves involved in that business — the business of cleaning up the dinner scraps and the dishes. But we went about it in pretty relaxed fashion. I thought the next move would be getting Henrietta fixed for the night. But there's a strange and very real fact. Things never work out quite as you think.

Suddenly Aunt Em said, "Well, Elmer, what about tomorrow?"

"Why tomorrow . . . tomorrow, I suppose we'll start for home, just as planned. I don't see any reason to postpone it, do you, Em?"

"That's exactly what I am talking about." We all stood and looked at her, pretty blankly I expect, because it didn't seem to us that she was talking about leaving at all. "All of us need to get a good bath, now don't we? Here we've been roaming about these hills, riding bears and stomping through the brush. Obviously we need a bath."

And she looked around at us all fiercely as if expecting us to deny it. Only nobody could. "Oh, that, Em. Well, there are shower facilities here at the camp ground," said Uncle Elmer. "You're making such a big thing out of it that I thought for sure you had some momentous undertaking in mind. But we can all go up to the camp facilities. They have public showers here, you know."

"But that's exactly what I AM talking about. Have you seen those facilities? When they say public, they mean public. They've got the shower in the women's section set up right in the middle of the room. Now at Jenny's age, it maybe doesn't matter. But I'm expecting you, Elmer, to figure out something to give me a bit of privacy. I do not aim to put on any public spectacle."

The idea of Aunt Em being a public spectacle made all of us kids snicker. And she glared at us mighty fiercely again. Uncle Elmer started to say something and then he stopped short. When someone as old as Aunt Em makes up her mind, you might as well forget about trying to change it with words. I guess Uncle Elmer knew this better than any of us. So he sat there and thought and nodded his head. Then he said, "Let's take a ride." Just like that.

"Elmer, have you taken leave of your senses? Take a ride? We're going to get all the riding we need tomorrow."

"That may be true, but if you want a private shower, you'll have to take a ride first."

Aunt Em wanted to argue. She set her jaw in a way that usually indicated the start of an argument. But she didn't. She just huffed her way to Henrietta and climbed in. So did we all. And away we went. Not far. Only as far as the shore of the lake. And there Uncle Elmer stopped the car.

"Now, Em," he said, "before we go to all the trouble of setting things up for you, private like, you'll have to understand that this will be a cold shower . . . seeing as how the water's coming out of that lake."

"A cold shower's better than a public one. So go ahead," she said.

Right away Uncle Elmer had us all working. He had Pete and me haul down the tarps that were covering the luggage. The same tarps that we had rigged up for a sail that one night. Then he found a hoop of wire and threaded those tarps onto the hoop. We saw what he had then — a shower stall, camping style. While we were working at this, Jenny screwed a length of hose to the place under the radiator. Uncle

Elmer helped her carefully lay it down to the lake. He was very particular that the end of the hose lay near the surface of the water where it might be a little warmer. Next he pulled out a length of pipe and to this he attached a shower head. I tell you, Uncle Elmer seemed to be ready for almost any emergency. He put the hoop with the tarps on top of the pipe. Then he stuck the pipe in the top of the radiator. And there! presto, a private shower.

Aunt Em eyed it a mite suspiciously. She was always awfully mistrusting of Henrietta. Which seemed very strange when you think of all the times that Henrietta had given us a hand — a real helping hand. Or maybe that's the wrong word? Anyway, Pete followed Uncle Elmer's instructions and started the engine. Aunt Em walked to the front of the car and fumbled around in the folds of the tarp trying to find the way in. She finally found the ends of the cloth and slipped through. That opening was right at the front. We could hear her laying things on Henrietta's hood. A few moments later she sang out, "Let 'er rip."

"What do I do now, Uncle Elmer?" yelled Pete.

"Push the orange button with S on it," said Uncle Elmer.

So Pete did. There was a rush of water and funny little squeals from behind the tarp when the first cold blast hit. Then Aunt Em began singing in her cracked, off-key voice and mixed in with these sounds were familiar ones of scrubbing. Uncle Elmer walked away and sat down on a rock, looking off at the rising

moon. Jenny was on the shore tossing in pebbles. I
don't know what's so fascinating about that game, but
it is intriguing to watch the ripples spread out and out
and out till they vanish. Pete got tired of sitting in
Henrietta so he went to join Jenny tossing rocks. And
from underneath the tarp, water ran out and the
ground got a muddy look.

"Elmer . . ." That was Aunt Em. "Back Henrietta
up a mite. It's getting muddy. And you can turn her
off too."

Uncle Elmer nodded at me to do this. So I did. I
don't know what happened next. I backed her up, set
the brake and turned off the engine as I'd been told.
I'm sure that I set that brake. Aunt Em yelled for
her towel which I saw lying on the front seat. So
maybe in reaching over to get the towel and clamber
out, I knocked the brake off. But this I know for certain sure. That brake got released somehow. 'Course,
I didn't know it then. I took the towel to the front of
Henrietta where Aunt Em's bony arm was waving
through the tarps, and I dropped the towel in her waving fingers. It disappeared.

For a moment I stopped right where I was to con-
sider what to do next. I had about decided to join Pete
and Jenny in their rock tossing when I felt this nudge.
Something was leaning mighty hard against the back
of my knee. I turned around to look and jumping jelly
beans! it was Henrietta's bumper pushing against me.
Now it seems reasonable that you ought to be able to
hold back a car, but when that car's on an incline and

you've got mud under your feet, you have a real problem. I turned around and shoved with my shoulder
against the part of the radiator not covered by tarp.

"Stop shoving . . . you hear me? Stop shoving!"
That was Aunt Em's voice. So I stopped shoving. An
order is an order. Only a minute later I realized that
Aunt Em had been shouting at Henrietta — not me.
By then it was too late. Because Henrietta, once I
stopped leaning against her, really began to move forward. And as Henrietta moved, there was the patter of
feet running on dirt — that was Aunt Em. Then I
heard more thumping feet. And that was Uncle Elmer. He yelled, "Stop that car."

And I did try to. Honest, I did. I was closest, so I
raced after it and threw myself at the front door. But
I missed the handle. I think my feet slipped in the
mud which threw me backwards. One foot slid under
the car and I tell you, for a minute there, I thought the
stars had really fallen. As old Henrietta rolled over my
ankle there were all these queer flashes of light and
shapes in my brain. I guess pain can do that. Through
the curtain of flashing shapes, I saw that Henrietta
was sliding into the water. Uncle Elmer had hold of
her bumper. So did Pete. But the car had too much
momentum and kept right on going. After a moment
Uncle Elmer let go . . . he tugged Pete loose too.
And then I remembered. Uncle Elmer couldn't swim.
But where was Aunt Em? She couldn't swim either.

I began to run, a hopping, lumpety kind of run, because the ankle that Henrietta had tromped over felt

like it was exploding into jagged pieces. You never
really know what you can do until you have to do it.
That's what my Dad used to say. And I guess he was
right. Because even as I ran, I was shucking my heavy
sweater and struggling to get my jeans off. At the
water's edge I squinted out toward Henrietta as she
gently floated away from us. And dimly, I could see
that Aunt Em's head was sticking out between the
tarps. She looked like a figurehead on an old sailing
ship. I guess she must have jumped on the bumper
when they reached the water, and then slipped forward like that. It sure didn't look comfortable.

I didn't have the strength to tell anybody what I was going to do. I simply pulled off my shoes and plunged into the water in a racing dive. Wowee! it was like being dumped into a tub of ice water. For a moment I thought my blood would freeze and I'd go down like a piece of lead. But I didn't. My brain automatically kept signaling my legs and arms to kick and pull and I swam. It became automatic. The pain and the motion and the cold. It was lucky that I'd done some competition swimming because you learn to keep going there even though you think you can't swim another stroke. I think the terrible cold must have frozen the ankle so no more waves of pain hit me. And I kept moving towards that luminous shape that was Henrietta. When I reached her, I had to fumble in my thinking about what to do next. My brain seemed frozen. Then I thought about pulling myself up on the running board and started to do just that when I whacked my ankle on the metal edge. Waves of blackness washed across me. I almost fell off. But something seemed ordering me to turn the handle on the front door. I must have done that, because I remember half falling across the seat. It was warmer there. I thought of resting. Only I didn't dare. I had to keep going.

Lucky I was familiar with starting Henrietta because I couldn't seem to focus on things too well. There was a hazy quality to everything, including my thinking. I did the things I knew I should do and Henrietta responded with a comfortable roar from her engine. For a minute I sat there, the engine roaring and nothing happening. Then I heard Uncle Elmer shouting something about the B button. B is for Boat went through my foggy mind. I groped for a button and pushed. Whambo, over I went backwards. I thought for a moment that someone was laughing, and I knew for certain sure that it wasn't me. Groggily I pulled myself up, pushed another button, and the back of the seat came into place. Now I saw the B and pushed that. We started to move. I'll say. Right towards the edge of the dam. Aunt Em was screaming at me to "Do something," which was logical. She had reason to shout. I was beginning to get foggier. Then the voices from the shore penetrated the layers of fog. It was comfortable hearing those voices. I had the message. With a twist of the steering wheel I turned Henrietta back towards the shore and the figures standing there. It seemed to me, in a vague way, that there were an awful lot of shadows there for only Pete and Jenny and Uncle Elmer. After a bit they began to take shape . . . oh, lots of shapes as I got closer and some of them seemed to be wading out to meet us. They were shoving and shouting and pushing. And Henrietta was back on land. I sat there with the engine roaring and vaguely recognized that half the camp was there and the other half coming. They lifted Aunt Em off the bumper. She had this wild shower cap over her hair and was wrapped in a fuzzy red bathrobe. She looked awfully limp to me. Maybe she was dead. My heart contracted. Angrily I stomped

down on the brake and suddenly the hurt was there.
The screaming awful hurt. And I was gone. There was
a great black cloud of nothingness and I . . . I was
the biggest nothingness of all.

All Good Things Must? . . .

IT's hard to find words to describe that sensation of coming back from nowhere into somewhere. Now why do you suppose that an unconscious person is described as "coming to"? Coming to what? I've never figured that out. And let me tell you, using those words to describe what happened to me seemed like a pretty pale description of the confusions and thoughts and lost sensations. That dark place you go when you're unconscious isn't like sleep. It's like being lost in a black cave of nothingness. There's none of the comfort or warmth or coziness of sleep.

I was floating around in this nothingness when I heard a word and then a few other words. They didn't make much sense. And suddenly I was terribly afraid to come out of the darkness . . . afraid of what I might find. Oh, I didn't think this out, you know, but remember that the last time I'd been unconscious I'd come to and found my parents dead. Somehow those feelings of disaster and despair were with me again. I rejected consciousness. I clung to the dark nothingness.

So I didn't really become conscious until I was in the hospital room. There you are, things had come full circle again. All our adventures with the Pufferdinks had started from one hospital and now I had a terrible fear that they were ending in another. Aunt

Em must be dead. Only as I focused my eyes on the shapes in the room, I made out this streaked gray hair with the bun at the back and the crazy knitting needles bobbing and nodding from their perch in the bun. Aunt Em was sleeping in the chair by the window.

Boy! was I relieved. A great weight pulled itself off my heart and I suddenly felt like singing. But I didn't. People don't do the things they feel like very often. And there's a sad and very real truth. Instead I said, "Aunt Em . . . you all right, Aunt Em?"

She didn't answer me at all. But she seemed to snap to attention and lean over to Uncle Elmer. Why, there he was, nodding in another chair. "Elmer . . . Elmer . . . Chris is awake. The boy's awake."

Uncle Elmer woke up, but he did it pretty slowly. Suddenly he seemed old and sort of tired. Funny, even though I knew both he and Aunt Em were old, I never ever thought of them that way. They were both always doing such crazy, unpredictable things that I never tagged them as being any particular age at all. They were simply Aunt Em and Uncle Elmer. I was thinking through this idea when I realized that Uncle Elmer was standing there on one side of the bed and Aunt Em on the other. And they were beaming at me. It was such a darned happy beaming that I couldn't help but smile back at them.

"Chris, boy. You all right?" asked Uncle Elmer.

"Chris! Chris!" That was Aunt Em and she kept patting my knee as she said my name.

"Say, boy, what did you think of the cast? Surprised, eh? You never did come to. Not even when they set it. That doctor up there at camp shot you full of pain killer and you didn't even move once on the trip down here to the hospital."

No wonder I had been in a cave of dark nothingness. "What happened?" I asked.

"Nothing much, 'cept you're a hero. It's spread all over the papers. Why, we even got a call from *Life* Magazine. They want some pictures of you and Aunt Em and Henrietta. Actually, all of us. Think of that now," said Uncle Elmer.

"Me? A hero? You must be kidding." The idea struck me so funny that I laughed right out loud.

"Sure you're a hero. And I can't think of anyone more deserving of the title. Took real guts to leap into that ice water, what with your ankle broken in three places. Wonder you didn't drown." Uncle Elmer grinned at me with his funny lopsided grin. Boy, it really made me feel good.

"That Henrietta," said Aunt Em. "I tell you, that car is getting more notional all the time. Sometimes I get this queer feeling that she's a publicity hound. You can imagine what happened when this business in the lake came out."

"No, Aunt Em, what did happen?"

"Why, the sheriff down the road had to get in his two cents' worth about Henrietta's dishwashing and how he and Mr. Cory got attacked with flying dishes. Then somebody in Wall called in about the sailing object. And the Ranger had to notify the paper about my springing onto the bear. I'm almost embarrassed to step out on the street. People eye us as if we were some kinds of freaks."

"Gee, Aunt Em, Henrietta makes me feel good. It's better to feel good and be a freak than feel ungood and be normal, wouldn't you say?" and I was looking right at Uncle Elmer. I had a wonderful warm feeling of belonging. And suddenly I felt for certain sure that the Pufferdinks were going to keep us. We had a family at last.

Which shows how wrong you can get. Sometimes

you get wishing something so hard that it gets in the way of common sense. And there's a strange and very real fact. I only had to stay in the hospital about twenty-four hours. They had put this crazy walking cast on. Henrietta had really smashed my ankle, but good, when she'd rolled over it. But I didn't hold a grudge. After all, it was pretty stupid of me in the first place, to have slipped like that. Besides, Pete and Jenny acted so sweet and loving towards me that they inflated my ego to the size of a dirigible balloon. I was mighty puffed up about myself. And I came down to size pretty fast.

Because after all the picture-taking was over and the excitement of being interviewed had simmered down, we finally got back into Henrietta and started out of Rapid City, headed for home. We were riding along like that, quiet . . . just thinking . . . when Uncle Elmer said, "Well, kids, we've been saving the best news for the last."

Here it was. I could feel it coming. Uncle Elmer and Aunt Em had made up their minds, because they had discovered what really great kids we were. Wow! I was really impressed with us all, but mostly with me. I could hardly wait for him to get out the words that they were going to adopt us, official like. He went on. "Yes siree, bob!" He was talking to us over his shoulder, looking back every now and then. "Did you notice all those calls we got in the hospital? I told Em you couldn't help but wonder."

I kept wondering why he was taking such a long

time to get to the point. And actually, I hadn't noticed the calls at all. So much had been going on that I suppose I took the calls as natural. "Well," said Uncle Elmer, "all this publicity produced the miracle that Em and I have been secretly hoping for."

How he could call that affair in the lake a miracle was beyond me. But then people do get extravagant with words when they're really excited. And Uncle Elmer did seem unnaturally wound up. Like a coiled spring. Pete and Jenny bounced nervously. I was beginning to feel a little uneasy myself.

Uncle Elmer had stopped for a minute to read the road signs. Then he started in talking again. "You know your Mom had a favorite cousin, name of Martha Gillis. When your Mom came to visit us Marthy would be over and practically live with us too. They were about as close as real sisters. See, both of them were the only children in their family so they really ate up the fun of being together at our house. Marthy married and moved East and we lost track of her. Imagine our surprise to hear that she and her husband, Jim, had joined the Peace Corps. They had no children and got this urge to serve people in some way. She's a truly wonderful kind of person." He stopped again.

What was going on here? I felt like you do when you walk into the middle of a television movie. I couldn't seem to sort out the plot or characters. Uncle Elmer was trying to tell us something, but I sure as heck couldn't see what. And that scared me.

Then Uncle Elmer started talking again. And we were still on the subject of Martha Gillis and Jim. "See, the two of them were in Paris on their way home to the States when they saw the story about our little fracas. It was smack on the front page of the Paris edition of *The New York Times*. Naturally they were surprised. Stunned is more like it. Because Marthy didn't even know that your folks were dead. Let alone that the five of us and Henrietta were cavorting around the Black Hills."

Uncle Elmer was talking slower and slower and Henrietta was moving slower and slower. Both of them had lost their forward momentum. Aunt Em was sitting there on the front seat so stiff and quiet that the knitting needles in her hair didn't quiver a snitch. And her lips were pressed together tight as tight as if she didn't dare let out words. I felt like butterflies were chasing goose pimples up my backbone. And Jenny and Pete looked as scared as me.

"So Marthy called us on the telephone — that's just what she did. All the way from Paris. Coulda knocked Em and me over with a snow flake. Yessirree bob, we were that surprised. Hey, Em?"

"For mercy sakes, Elmer, get on with it. You're hemming and hawing and chawing along. About to drive me crazy. Spit it out. Quick like. That Marthy and Jim are coming back to her family's home in Prairie Junction. She's always held on to it even while they've been roaming the world. Her security insurance is what she called it. And she said to tell the Nelson kids that they could just count on being their family from now on. So there. It's said."

"THEIR FAMILY!" All of us got it out — somehow it came out together. But Jenny squalled it, Pete squawked and I squeaked. Crazy how things can happen to your voice.

"Galloping goose-eggs," yelled Pete, just as Uncle Elmer did when he was surprised, "who needs them? We've got you, Uncle Elmer, and Aunt Em and Petunia and Henrietta."

"Don't you love us, Aunt Em?" Jenny's voice had a little shake in it. She was about ready to cry.

"Sakes alive, honey. Don't ever get the idea we don't love you. Why, I couldn't even tell you how much Elmer and I love you young 'uns. You've put spice in our lives. But loving's not the only important thing. You have to do what's right."

"Then how could you think of letting us be their family?" I said. "That couldn't be right. Never, never, never."

"Uncle Elmer, we'll do anything! We'll be quiet and help and not fuss about chores and feed Petunia and wash Henrietta. Anything at all, if you'll just let us stay." That was Jenny.

Henrietta zigged right off the road and stopped on the shoulder. Uncle Elmer sort of swiped at his eyes with his sleeves. He seemed to be having trouble seeing or something. Maybe he was as upset as we were.

"It's like this . . ." And Uncle Elmer pulled out his red bandanna handkerchief and blew his nose like a trumpet. Whoooeee! I bet Henrietta almost shot off her tires at the sound. On the other hand, maybe she was used to it. But here's a strange thing: that loud, raucous noise sort of helped us get by the tense and frightening moment. Uncle Elmer cleared his throat and said, "It's not that you don't help, children. And not that we don't love you. It's because . . . well, think of the space teams."

"Elllmer, don't get off the subject," said Aunt Em, rather fiercely.

"I am not off the subject. Because raising these kids is every bit as important as a rocket shot to the moon. And space fliers always have a back-up team."

"So what?" said Pete. Boy, he was puzzled. Well, so was I.

"So Em and me, we need a back-up team too. And that's what Marthy and Jim are going to be. Our back-up team. Because something can happen. Oh, not anything awful or drastic. But just a little thing can happen where a body needs help. Another person ready to step in."

"They'd just better watch where they step," said Jenny. Which was such a crazy thing to say, and she said it in such a belligerent way, that I felt a laugh bubbling up. And there it came, a jiggledy kind of snicker. Jenny looked surprised, and then she couldn't help herself. She grinned back at me. But that old

Pete. He wouldn't smile. He plunged on. "Do we have to live with them?" The way he said it he almost made the "them" sound dirty.

"No," said Aunt Em. And she said it so sharply and loudly that Uncle Elmer jumped. "No, this year you'll be with us. Right, Elmer?"

And Uncle Elmer's shoulders seemed to perk up as if he liked what he was hearing. "Right, Em." He gave each of us one of his warm, crooked smiles. Then he shoved his bandanna back in his pocket and shifted Henrietta's gears. And that old gal sprang into action with so much zip that she threw us kids into a heap on the floor. "What about next year?" asked Pete as he pulled himself off the floor. "Huh, Uncle Elmer?" That kid could never let things lie peaceful like.

"Why, next year? We'll take care of next year when it comes," said Uncle Elmer. "Remember Pufferdink's law?"

"Enjoy the unexpected!" And this time we shouted it out with a happy sound.

"Right! Let next year take care of itself."

Which you have to admit was a pretty good piece of advice. Because you can worry and think and debate about tomorrow but it never has changed a thing. And that's a strange and very hard fact. Inside I felt like singing. We could count on this year with Aunt Em and Uncle Elmer and maybe next year and maybe even the year after that. So why worry.

The scenery began whirling by in its usual monotonous way. Jenny was hugging Petunia who didn't even seem to mind. And Pete had his eyes closed. Thinking, I suppose. So I did some thinking of my own. I thought that maybe Uncle Elmer was right and Henrietta's moonlight swim had spawned a miracle. Kind of a backward miracle. But it looked as if we were going to get some more family and, as I see it now, you can never have too much family. Then I had a wonderful idea. Just like that. What if Uncle Elmer and Aunt Em took us on another trip next summer? Would we have a whole bunch more of crazy, unpredictable adventures? The idea made me pause — then I grinned. How stupid can you get? Why surely never again could we have such delicious, delightful fun as we had had this year when Henrietta had gone West. And so had we.